THE IMPALPABLE TRAP

SOCIALIZING IS A SIN FOR HER

INJLA SHARIQ

Copyright © Injla Shariq
All Rights Reserved.

This book has been self-published with all reasonable efforts taken to make the material error-free by the author. No part of this book shall be used, reproduced in any manner whatsoever without written permission from the author, except in the case of brief quotations embodied in critical articles and reviews.

The Author of this book is solely responsible and liable for its content including but not limited to the views, representations, descriptions, statements, information, opinions and references ["Content"]. The Content of this book shall not constitute or be construed or deemed to reflect the opinion or expression of the Publisher or Editor. Neither the Publisher nor Editor endorse or approve the Content of this book or guarantee the reliability, accuracy or completeness of the Content published herein and do not make any representations or warranties of any kind, express or implied, including but not limited to the implied warranties of merchantability, fitness for a particular purpose. The Publisher and Editor shall not be liable whatsoever for any errors, omissions, whether such errors or omissions result from negligence, accident, or any other cause or claims for loss or damages of any kind, including without limitation, indirect or consequential loss or damage arising out of use, inability to use, or about the reliability, accuracy or sufficiency of the information contained in this book.

Made with ❤ on the Notion Press Platform
www.notionpress.com

To all the girls--

you don't need an XY to steady your steps, nor a burrowed name to write your worth. You were born whole, fierce in silence, and enough - always enough.

Contents

Contents

ACKNOWLEDGEMENTS

Thankyou God for giving me strength and the right path.

I am wholeheartedly thankful to my sister, whose thoughtful insights and late night conversations enriched, my understanding on countless topics specially our cherished discussions on feminist issues.

To my Lil brother, Shazain whose innocent mischiefs and affection continues to brighten my days, though he did choose the Air Conditioned over ME!

To my Father, Mirza Shariq Baig, whose tireless effoerts and silent struggles inspire me every single day, I LOVE YOU PAPA!

To my Mother, Dr. Farah Deeba, whose discipline is appreciable yet whose wit never fails to bring smile. Her presence is a remarkable balance of strength and humour.

Though they may express it differently, I know both my parents love us deeply. That indeed, is the beautiful irony.

I amdeeply thankful to Ma'am Reeta Mathur, MPS International School, Jaipur(Raj.) whose constant faith in me has always served as alight in moments of uncertainity. Love you ma'am!

My sincere appreciation also goes to my Principal Ma'am and the entire Maheshwari Samaj Jaipur, for their unwavering dedication to fostering value based education. Their support in nurtring a strong academic environment enabled me to find the courage to write this book.

Lastly, inspired by brilliant Apoorva Mukhija, I discovered the fire of **IDC** within myself, and learned how to hold my ground with grace, even in nthe face of toughest critics.

I extend my respect and gratitude to my Grand parents, family and all relatives- Maternal and Paternal.
Most Importantly -- Me MYSELF :}

FOREWORD

I've known the weight of invisible chains ---money struggles, family walls, and later, a cage I walked into myself. I stayed for love, but found humiliation, threats, and pain instead.

This book is my escape. My voice. My truth

Impalpable Trap is more than a story --it's a cry for freedom, from everything that ever tried to silence me. If you've ever felt trapped, may these pages remind you that even the quietest fight matters --and freedom, though fragile, is always worth chasing.

~ Injla
Student, Class XII
MPS International School, Jaipur, Raj.

PREFACE

Have you ever wondered how it feels like being trapped? Let's think of even worse situation, You are trapped and the keys to the lock are lost, you do not know how that key looks like or where it is.... and now! Just imagine, if this trap can not be seen by others.. you are alone and lonely. Insecurity hugs you so tightly.

This little girl, waits for the key every single day.

IMPALPABLE TRAP

shhhhhhhhhhhhh!!!!
     did you heard that?
     keep queit and try to focus ,
     DId not hear it even after focusing?
     yes, Her cries are not heard by any of us, she cries silently
and calm herself silently.
     Let me tell you about her...
     Maybe you will hear her cries in the end.

PROLOGUE

Dark and disturbing winds, hitting and murdering many plants. Pushes back a lady, struggling to make her way through those disturbing gales.

The lady was looking hard working, shaking and protecting a fresh human baby.

Suddenly sky started to cry.

ommo... do you need any help?

no... i will handle this..[heavy breathe]

Aiguuu... i will take her.

She snatched the baby and ran, leaving her temperory footseteps and lifeless hardworking lady behind...............

I

A calm and soothing evening, Kids running out from houses, winds of relaxation covered the whole environment, chukles and giggles of those young humans, discussing "what should we play today?" "lets play hide and seek!"

"kids playing games after completing their chores, most relaxing moment ever. But someone cannot enjoy like this."

the environment was too good to swallow, to feel that environment as the way it is for someone. That someone who was enduring the play of those young ones, running and playing, sweat of joys, deep tiring breathes of amusement,Frivolous rebukes, as if their cloud, the bond was unbreakable, by deep black and lonely eyes of that calm and mysterious girl,faked a barbaric expression on her face, totally lost in figuring out the environment created by the amusing acts of those young ones, maybe she never had those rebukes, maybe she had never expirienced how a fun activity with friends after completing all the task assign feels like. Smira, was standing on the balcony, hands holding the old rusting railing and tried to feel the enjoyment of those kids.

> "*Smira is a calm and mysterious girl. She stood still at the balcony. she was not allowed to step outside. she had never experience the things and enjoyment the other kids do. She always had a poker face, never smiled heartily.*"

"Smira! do NOT stand on that balcony! how many times do i have to repeat my instructions!? come here!"

a barbaric voice came. It was the voice of her mother.

Her mother is unexplainable. She had sevre punishments even for minute acts done by Smira. Like, standing in the balcony. Smira closed the balcony door and slowly came to her mother. Calmly accepting her punishment.

"Go! wash the dishes!" Smira went in the kitchen. There was a whole stack of dirty..... extremely dirty dishes. Smira wore dish washing gloves. "Who told you to wear those? did i?" her mother said in a scaring sarcastic manner.

Smira washed all the dishes without the gloves. She was grossing out. But could not do anything. After washing those dishes she saw her hands, rough... a lot rough. she went in her room and sat on her bed. while scratching her rough hands, she had a deep sigh.

She looked out of the window, it was incomplete black sky. she looked up in the sky, there were no stars

she whispered "Are they also trapped?"

She heard footsteps of her mother. She quickly pretended to sleep.

her mother entered and said "pack your school bag! tomorrow you will be going to school!" Smira got up. She was happy,but she got sad after she heard her mother's instructions.

Next day,

She woke up, a completely new day! but not for her. The thing added was now she could go to school. But as she had not meet anyone or talked to anyone. She had a huge problem in socializing.

She sat in the car.Her mother drove her, on the way she saw something. she said, Smira! see that girl? " Smira looked at her. Smira said " yes mother.." "dont talk to her ever!" Smira slowly said ".......why.......?" "Do you want a punishment again? your hairs are looking so beautiful nowadays.. " " sorry mother.... i will obey you" Smira quickly said. Her mother continued " see... that girl's character is not good! she is surrounded with boys!" when Smira looked, she percieved it as a normal thing. Having male friends is not bad.

She said" yes mother.. you are right." in a reluctant manner.

Smira entered the school. Looking everything in a discriptive way. She endured, fight among students in corridor, girls wearing make up, gatherings of students. She was confused and a little scared. She was experiencing all this for the first time.

She stepped in the class, so nervous and confused. Stood beside the teacher looking down at the floor. "Smira, introduce yourself." asked the teacher. Smira's beautiful but nervous eyes looked up. All eyes were on her."h...hel....hello... i...i... am s..s..smira.." "Hi, Smira.. everyone greeted back. students were happy seeing Smira.

Smira went in the last and sat there.

"it looks like..she loves the me time of her, or..... it is because of her mother, who keeps her in the dark, away from the world. just like the princess locked from outer world, Trapped in the room. But the day she went to school, a door of freedom slightly opened in her life full of impalpable traps."

II

"Hi, Smira! myself Alice" Smira looked at her and responded "who...who are you?"

Alice laughed,/ "seriously?!!?" Smira felt awkward. she thought....

"she is the girl, mother warned me about.."

Smira started ghosting Alice. Alice sat beside her. Smira thought..........

"damn it!! why is she here!! go away!"

Smira wanted Alice to leave her so badly, to find a solution of this situation she looked at the door side of the noisy class room. Her eyes encountered a boy, pointing towards Alice. Smira did not even think, as if it was a nice opportunity to get rid of Alice. Quickly words came out from her excited and quick mouth, "someone's calling you.." Alice looked there and exclaimed " ohh! John!! come over!!"

"Mother's gonna kill me! i need to get out from here!! uhhh!! why did she came to me!!!?"

Smira stood up and said stuttering " i....i....i..... want to go to the restroom..." Smira quickly left.

John came.

Alice said in deep thinking " is she uncomfortable with me?" she looked at John and said " i think she does not like me..."

John laughed.

"who would ever like you!!??" Alice punched his back and left saying " SHUT UP!"

Smira was standing at corridor, staring an ant.

"*What a lucky creature!*"

Smira made a trap from her hands around the ant. Ant crawled over her hand.

"What happened?" Alice said.

Smira got embarassed. She quickly stood straight. Alice said "Woa!! were you trapping a small innocent creature?" Smira was quiet.

Alice looked up in the sky and said "one reflect the things which are suffered by them in any means." Smira looked at her and headed towards the class.

"You are that small and innocent creature! trapped!"

Smira was very surprised. The ground slipped beneath her feet. She had a unique chilling feeling. She turned back, Alice came close to her and said " see..... i am not a bad one... you can share things with me... you can be my friend...." Smira said" h.....h....how... d...d.. do you k..k..know?.... that i.....i..... am that creature... who is trapped.....?"

Alice said "Anyone can see... its obvious, you haven't even stepped in the world." Smira said "But it's dangerous! and i will obey my mother!" she left. Alice stood still.

CLASS BEGINs....

No one was interested in the class. Every was was tired and reluctant in studying. Well who will be concentrating after a nice break, fun and enjoyment with friends.

Teacher entered and asked students to take out books and open page no. 40.....

Smira was not able to concentrate at all because of the things Alice had said to her were going on in her squandered mind.

"Maybe Alice is right. Mother is a bit strict. She does not give me freedom. Should i talk to her. no.....no..... she is always ready with a punishment." She controlled herself and thought....

"NO... my mother is right.. that girl is characterless!!
i need to stay away from her!!"

Teacher wandered in the class, he saw an empty bench " who sits here!? why isn't they present? i guess break is over right?"

"John!" answered the chorus.

"Alice,Why hasn't your brother come yet? where has he gone?"

This sentance knocked Smira's socks off. She was so shocked.

"Sir, I..I do not know where he had gone. sorry sir" Alice answered..

After the class was over,

Alice was packing her stuff. Smira silently stood beside her, Alice looked at her and said "ohh hi.. Smira.." Smira looked down in guilt and slowly said "i am sorry..." Alice was confused.

"i...i... thought you..you are bad..... and that.....John is not your brother.... he is....."

" SHUT UP!!!! EWWWWW Seriously......" Alice cringed out.

"How could you imagine that..? its disgusting!"

Smira again apologized. Alice hugged her and said " lets walk home together..." Smira was happy as the cloud of guilt vanished. But she was sad, this incident will not be able to change her mother's thinking.

Smira needs to be alert now.

III

Smira and Alice were walking together, Smira was little worried......

"*if mother finds this out.... she would kill me.. or would come up with a severe punishment!*"

What was feared, has happened! Smira's mother saw her walking with Alice. She went to them with bursting anger and scratched Smira's hand with her long nails and pulled her. "I warned you!" "YOU SHOULD HAVE LISTEN TO MY WORDS AND OBEY ME!" Smira was scared what punishment will she go through this time.

"*you never knew the truth of her! how could you judge so easily!*"

On the way, Smira was getting mentally prepared for the punishment.
    Phone rings.
Smira's mother picked it up and stopped the car.
She got out of the car.

Smira was watching her mother's action they were wierd.

Smira thought.....

"Mother acts wierd all the time when she talks on phone, who is the person which makes her mood so good.. last time when i mistakenly slept in her room... i was saved by that person... who could it be?"

After some time...

They reached home..

Smira went in her room silently. Her mother was happy

Smira sat on her bed and sighed. "Am i grounded?" She put her head down thinking that she is been grounded..

"Is it necessary to be so isolated?"

"hello.... i am Ms. Amanda.... teacher you talked to....."

"ohhh.... yes! she is upstairs..."

"ohh..ok.. i will follow my lead then"

"WAIT! you cannot take any kind of gadget! submit your phone here!"

knock knock

"Hello.. there.."

"I am your home teacher..."

Smira looked back.

And said reluctantly,"Home schooling.....again....."

Ms. Amanda came and sat beside her...

She started with the lesson..

"So... the topic name is.... motion... well you will study it in detail in your higher classes,i will give you an idea what is it.. ok..?"

Smira was not interested.

She was listening to her with no expressions..

"We all have travelled in train, car or in any land vehicle.. so....."

"i have never...."

Ms. Amanda stopped she asked"w..what..?" she was confused..

Smira continued "today was the first and last time i travelled in the car."

Ms. Amanda went in deep thoughts.. She was confused and surprised.. She laughed to make the situation light and she changed the topic

"Let us study IT... you have mobile phone.. right.. have you wondered how it functions? or have you operated a laptop or a computer??"

"NO... NEVER... I have seen phone but never operated... and rest i have neither touched nor saw them.."

Ms. Amanda felt a little wrong. She thought.....

"how could any kid nowadays, don't know what's electronics!!!? is she really isolated from the world? why is her mother doing so??"

Ms Amanda looked at the wall and searched the clock..

"You won't find anything... I don't have a wall clock.."

"i just stay in my room.. i have no connections to the outer world... i have this little window.. but i have to lock it all the time as per my mother's order..."

Ms. Amanda was so shocked..

"how could any mother lock her own daughter!!? if she won't be allowed to go outside.. she will never be able to face the world.. there will be lot's of lacking in her.. it cant be..... i need to do something..."

After Ms. Amanda left..

"SMIRA!!! COME HERE!!!" Smira went down..

"Go... wash the dishes.." Smira went in the kitchen and started washing the dishes...

while washing the dishes... she had a thought of looking for a phone...

After washing the dishes.. she went in her mother's room and searched phone.. she was slowly and silently searching for the phone.. She was also scared a little...

"WHAT ARE YOU DOING HERE??"

IV

Smira's breathe struck for a second, she turned back and said "m...m...mother.... I am looking for my notebook...."

"WHY!!?"

"i....it..it's l...lost..."

"HOW DARE YOU LOST IT?"

Smira looked down. She was scared.

You know your punishment! go and bring that!!

Smira was startled...

she cried "mother... i am sorry... spare me this time... i am really sorry!! i won't repeat it again!"

do as i say!! or your punishment will get more severe!!

Poor and scared Smira went and came back with sharp and shining metallic scissors. Her mother pushed her to the ground and started cutting her beautiful long brown locks.

Smira was crying silently.. tears rolled down her pink cheeks.. Regretting her life.

if you again made silly mistake like this.... i will make sure there won't be a single hair left on your scalp!

She rubbed Smira's cheeks lightly and said "my beautiful... daughter"

This was a creepy act by her mother.

Smira looked herself in the mirror, and cried so much

whole night was a sad and crying one for her..

She spent the night in regretting. Well what else this innocent soul could do.

She tortured herself in the bathroom.. Washed her face a lot of times

> *"my mother have different beliefs? or its just she wants to torture me.. but why only me..? what did i do wrong?"*

she heard footsteps...

she quickly made herself nice and fresh, opened the lock of the room's door and pretended to study. "dear are you studying?" Smira nodded.

"ohk... tomorrow is your test... if you did not performed well... you know what you will get right..?"

Smira sadly nodded

"i will try mother..."

her mother came close to her and softly touched her hairs saying "your hairs are long, even after cutting them..."

Smira was shivering but yet silent and calm outside..

"do you want these hairs to die?..... forever?..." Smira had tears in her eyes, she slowly said " sorry...... m.... m....mother.."

do not leave me in MAYBE situation! i hate to hear no!"

"yes mother..." Smira agreed.

She realized her mother is becoming harsh day by day. But she had no choice.

There was not any key for the trap.

she had to co-operate with her evil mother.

She was not allowed to socialize, make friends, go out, explore.

All she had was her room's tiny window.

She stared the moon and the stars.

"will i be able to see them from an open land?"

V

knock.....knock...

may i come in?

Ms. Amanda entered and said "so...are you ready for the test? Smira was still.

After a while,

Ms Amanda took her notebook. It was all blank. She softly rubbed Smira's back and said, "honey..are you not well..?"

Smira looked at her and swallowed,

She said, 'i want to use it.....The phone..."

Ms Amanda felt unreal.

She said,"It is..... it is a device... we can do many things from this device."

Smira questioned "like what!?"

"we can talk to friends....family.... we can search many things.... we can install interesting and knowledgeable applications...... and many more"

"but........"

"it is addictive, do not use it beyond limits..."

"do not worry.... i will not use phone... i do not have friends, family, i do not need any kind of applications.. and if i would have all these... i would not be allowed to use that.... just like now..."

Ms. Amanda was speechless...

Smira got alert. {she heard footsteps of her mother}

"what happened?" Ms. Amanda asked.

"mother...mother is coming.."

The door opened, Her mother enterred and said,'How much did she scored?"

Ms Amanda started speaking stammering, She looked at Smira and then at her mother.

Her mother snatched the notebook from Ms. Amanda's hand, it was all empty.

Ms. Amanda lied "test was not started yet! her mother said "what were you doing till now? wasting time!?"

Smira looked at Ms. Amanda,

"why is she lying? my mother's gonna kill her!"

Ms.Amanda stood up and said "I....I....."

"she was clearing my doubt... m...m..mother....."

Smira's stammering voice came.

Ms. Amanda was surprised. Her mother smirked and said " if it is true... good for you both! and if it is not......Smira darling... you know right!!your hairs are so beautiful!"

Smira slightly nodded. She was a little scared.

Her mother left saying "you! come downstairs!"

Ms. Amanda knelt down, she said "Why did you lied?"

Smira said " same question for you.."

Ms.Amanda smiled. She said "it is bad to lie! do not lie! ok!" Smira holded her hand and said "Can you do me a favor....?"

'Sure.....'

Smira slowly said " i want to use a phone" "but.. you have no interest in it.. right..?"

"i....i.... am just a little curious..."

Ms.Amanda said " ok... but it would be the first and last time.. ok..?"

Smira happily nodded

Ms. Amanda went downstairs and sneaked out the phone. She knocked Smira's door and enterred.

"here's a phone, when i will come tomorrow, i will take it!"

she left.

Smira was delighted

VI

Entire night was a beautiful daydream for Smira.

She was looking at phone and admiring the morphollogy of it. Her exciting fingers clicked the power button to switch on the phone.

She started exploring the phone.... Her eyes shined so bright as if she is standing before a lovely thing. It was a very joyful expirience for her.

She had a smile on her face while exploring the phone, as if all the gloom in her life was faded.

She clicked on *google,* and searched *friend.*

After she saw the results.. Smira was very excited and surprised.

"With this.... no one needs a teacher! no one needs to have a company!"

"woahhh!it is so magical!"

She clicked on camera and got JUMPSCARE... After looking her reflection on the screen "Ommooo!!! That was a mini heart attack.."

"It has a mirror also.. but i am looking a little different..."

"Haiiiissshhhhh why mother did not allowed me to see or use this kind of stuff... I will not misuse it.. "

Whole night was spent on watching vedios on youtube.. well she learned many good things too...

In the morning,

Ms. Amanda enterred the house.

Smira's mother stopped her and said "you.....are a teacher.." "Your life must be stressfull..."

Ms. Amanda said stammering "n...n...not really...."

'awkward laugh'

Smira's mother wandered in the garden saying "are you frustrated Ms Amanda?"

"A little we can say.."

again an awkward laugh....

Smira's mother started trimming the plants with secateurs.

"These are my favourite.. i just bought one of them... i wish i could buy all of them... but i had no choice..."

Ms. Amanda said "ohhhhhh.... yes.. these plants are so beautiful...they have health benefits also..."

"The Secateurs."

"W..What..?" Ms. Amanda asked.

"I was talking about the secateurs..."

Ms. Amanda stood still. She was not able to understand how to react...

"what doubt Smira asked you the previous day?"

Ms. Amanda was still processing. She came out of her processing and said"w..what..... pardon..?"

Smira's mother stood up and looked at Ms. Amanda..

Ms.Amanda said" sh..sh..she asked me.. how co...computer s..starts..."

Smira's mother smirked. She said "how strange.. Smira told me that she asked something related to Science.."

Ms. Amanda freaked out.

Sweat rolled over her body.. She said in a scared voice, "y..y....ye.."

"*SPLASH!!!!!!*"

Dark red blood splashed all over Smira's mother. The sharp tool was inside Ms Amanda!

"DO YOU EVEN HAVE ANY IDEA ABOUT WHAT YOU HAVE DONE!"

"YOU HAVE DONE THREE BIG CRIMES!"

"FIRST, YOU GAVE SMIRA THE PHONE! having phone is like a hell for her!!"

"SECOND, BECAUSE OF YOU SHE STARTED LYING! even after she know the result of her act, her punishment..! you played with my style of parenting..!"

"Third, AFTER ALL THESE CRIMES, YOU HAD GUTTS TO SHOW YOURSELF! and because of these crimes you are going to be gone...forever!"

Ms. Amanda slowly said in pain, "you.... are..... a monster..... not a mo.....mother..." and she fell down.

Smira's mother fixed her hairs and said, "yes....I am... a MONSTER MOTHER.."

After clearing up what she did.. she went to Smira.

Smira was little confused.

Her mother came to her with sharp scissors hiding at back.

suddenly, she got a call.. She looked at Smira and said" you are lucky.." and left.

Smira was very confused she recalled that earlier also, a phone call saved her from severe punishment. Who calls her, Whom she talks to and gets very happy..?"

Her mother came back and said " i am warning you.. Dare you go against my parenting!" Smira nodded.

Her mother left saying,"you are locked in this room for three days!"

Smira was sad.

she quickly asked,"what about home school?"

Her mother left saying.....

she won't come

VII

Room was dark, not only because of dim light, Smira's thoughts were also dark and negative.

"what happened to Ms Amanda?"

"She left the job on purpose.. or..... mother did something?"

She stood up and took out the phone, her body was shivering slightly, Her fingers quivered, Although it was useless.. she is a scaresick cat. Ofcourse, what you expect from a trapped and caged girl, who have never seen even a little view of outside world, the barbaric situations, deceitful people and heart breaks, butterflies, happiness, excitement, and many more. Only adjective she had was confused and a58 lame lifestyle.

LIGHT sparkled of phone's screen, She searched," How to escape?" Out of so many unsolved questions, she asked this useless question. Whole night spent doing escaping research.

She did not sensed that when she fall asleep, And dreamt something....something so sad for her,

"hi friends! hi Smira! let us play!!

Smira enjoyed like a normal kid, going out with friends, laughing, joking around, frivolous talks, Ectasted feeling blossom up.

Smira! Smira! WHERE ARE YOU!!??

Sorceress type voice ecoed. It was her evil mother.. Smira's sweat rolled over her forehead, she spontaneusly left the place and ran as far as she could. After so many steps she hid in a building.

what are you doing?

Smira glanced back, a young lad pulled over the blanket from their baddy face, messy hairs and unbothered eyes. Smira looked at them, but couldn't saw their face, a bright light sparked on their face.

Have you seen a ghost?

w...w....w....what....?

Why are you shivering like this?

Smira stood up, she said stutteringly, no....no....not.....noth....nothi....

Will you spend the whole night saying a single word completely..?

What did you saw..?

Smira Turned back and......

Her MOTHER KILLED BOTH OF THEM....

i told you not to socialize yourself dear, kissed her forehead

mumma loves you very much. Have a nice sleep."

Alarming dream she had.

She woke up hastily, She was blood curdling. She threw all the staff from table, shivering and scared walk towards her bathroom. She had a trimorous look in her mirror.

Opened the tap and splashed the water on her face, but it was like adding water in acid, Her creeps did not changed.

Phone rang

she got a jumpscare, she slowly went to the phone and unwittingly answered the call, "hello...hello......hello... mother! where are you!!?"

It must be Ms. Amanda's daughter. How should i inform her about Ms. Amanda. Where are you Ms Amanda..!?

Smira had intrapersonal communication.

"Hello.. Hello...Hello.... what's wrong with the phone..? Mom!!! Look!!!!! John is disturbing me!!!! Where are you!!!! When will you come..?"

"Mom I am not disturbing her, she hit me first!"6

"when did i hit you.. You......."

"Mom come fast!!!!!"

Smira was still, she said, "hello..?"

"hello.. mom..??"

"your mom left the phone at her workplace,"

"who are you..?"

"Sm...Sm..." she was not able to say the truth and the lie!

"Smira is that you..?" Smira was shocked.

"Smira...? it's me.. Alice..."

"Smira! I missed you so much! in which school are you studying right now..? ohh wait, my mother told us about you... you don't go out of your house! Mom talks about you alot, i sometimes feels jealous. But you deserve that much love she gives you <chuckles> Where is mother..?"

DISMAYED

Phone slept from perspiring hands in fear and shockness.

She heard something falling, she had a sneaky look, And she freezed.

Her mother was burrying a body with a man.

This was Smira's first explosure to the word "ADVENTURE".

Goosebumps covered her timid body all over, " Mother.... what is she doing? with that stranger...?" " who's body is she burrying?"

Smira stepped out of her room and went near the backyard door. She stood there and heard the conversation.. Thoughts were growing rapidly," who is that man? is he the man who calls and mother's mood gets happy? is... is..... is... that body of......"

Ms. AMANDA!!!

VIII

It was Smira's first time to be so bold and fearless. Although she was having chills inside, but her legs did not bothered to stop. She passed the horror corridor and reached the backyard door, she was a stone throw distance from her mother and that creepy man. The man was having bad vibes, and now that Smira was so close to them she could feel it very strongly. The man's face was reminding Smira of ugly lizard.

The man was wearing a shirt which was old, as the colour was fading out. His pants were torn, as if someone scrached him. His figure was not so good, His looks were distorted, a total grotesque he was.

Smira was enduring the scene even though she was broken out in cold sweat. She saw her mother putting down the body without any tension or stress of getting caught. The man pushed the body inside the pit they had just dug. Their eyes were so bold as if they were proud of their act. Not having a little console or grief of whatever they had done with Ms. Amanda. Smira closed her eyes in pain and griefy tears rolled down over her innocent cheeks. She reminisce herself with Ms.Amanda and thinking about what answer she will give to Alice.

"It's all because of me! why the heck i wanted to use phone! this useless phone destroyed the life of Ms. Amanda and her family! haisshhhh.. why....why..why..?"
Thinking and crying.

She looked at her mother and that lizard faced man. They had a conversation after they burried Ms.Amanda's dead body. "Now what are you going to do next.?" Her mother replied,"nothing.. live my life as normal." The man said,"police will come to know in a day or two.. and your daughter will come to know about this."

Her mother said," so what should i need to do..?"

The man said,"Send her somewhwere until this matter is fully solved!" Smira was listening.

her mother said,"no... i will not send her anywhere.. never!!!"

The man said " chill.. why are you acting like as if she is your own daughter!"

This dialogue of the man came like a bolt from the blue to Smira.

Her mother smirked and said,"i am her real mother! and i will keep her with me even if i need her to be caged!"

The man said," do not forget you had kidnapped her and killed her real mother! and if you need her to live with you, send her somewhere only for the time being."

This was too much to swallow and digest for Smira. She slowly went to her room, locked the door and sat with a jerk.

she was lost.

There was enough stress to stress. She was not able to figure out, where to grief.

"She....she....she... is not my real mother..?"

Smira's laugh burst out. It was not normal, she was laughing so hard that tears came out from beautiful organs which help her to see the things, But failed to see the fact that her mother was not her real mother.

She had always followed her mothers order, thinking she should obey her mother. Even after sevre punishment she forgive her mother because she had a thought that her mother is her real mother.

She was laughing so hard. She had not laughed this much before, even she was not aware how to laugh. she went in the bathroom and washed her face. Tied her small yet cool hairs.

She sat and planned.

"now that she is not my real mother, i can escape from this trap! i just need to prepare for this."

"SMIRA! SMIRA! COME DOWN!"

Smira said,"she thinks that i will obey her after knowing that she is not my real mother..?"

She went down and there was drastic change in her attitude.

She said, "what..?" it was a cold response. Her mother said,"do you want to die..?" Smira ranted in her own mind,"do you have that much gutts.?" Her mother came close to her and said,"speak! speak the shit ou of your damn mouth!" Smira did not spoke a word.

Her mother's anger volcano erupted,

She asked the man to grab her. Smira ranted again,"you both are just cheap fools. and you.... Sorry to say but you really look like a beggar! see your dressing style, our street dog looks better than you! Ugly lizard face you got! bruh... who would ever like you!? And this lady over here who treats like a cool and mysterious evil, nah evil!! you are a cheap blind. You like this ugly lizard faced man. haisshhh you both are cheap jokers. My eyes hurts seeing you." But she was struggling to speak them out. Obviously she was scared of her evil mother. After seeing her mother, she turned into a timid one. When that creep grabbed her, After two trials of get away from him, she got tired and gave up.

And her monster mother gave her a painful slap, her hairs jumped over her face and the white skin turned into red. But her expressions never changed a bit.

The creep released her.

"Smira... he is Uncle Liza.." "he is your future father.." Smira give him looks,

just as i thought this lady is blind, so much blind. What is the name of this mister? Is he the mistress, or his parents also think he looks like a lizard, and that also an ugly one. That is why he is named as lizard's short form, LIZArd.

She had a poker face.

The man, uncle Liza said,"oh dear, you are so pretty. Look at that innocent features you carry." He came close to Smira. Smira stepped behind. She looked at her mother, not her real mother with helping eyes. Her mother had an evil smile on that gross face of hers.

Smira was helpless, could not control her savage statement, "i doubt your earnings." the man stopped and said,"what..?" Smira looked at her mother, looking very gross. Wretchedness was dripping from her face. Smira slowly said,"I...i....mean...even a poverty stricken person is aware of grooming. But...you..you.." Her mother shouted,"WHAT!!?"

"YOUR BREATHE STINKS! ATLEAST YOU SHOULD HAVE BRUSHED YOUR TEETH! YOU GROSS OUT!"

Smira shouted and said very quickly. For the first time she said someting like this and in this manner. Although she was aware of what will happen to her. Her mother, not her mother smirked and said, " my parenting.... is this allowed my dear? you are awrae of your punishment.

right.?" Smira did not regret whatever she said. Instead she was covered with a feel of complacency.

Smira looked down to act as if she was guilty. The man,uncle Liza said,"ok... i will brush.." Smira controlled her laugh. She was amazingly good at this act. As whole life she had a poker face, she is brilliant in making that face. Her mother,not her mother shouted,"WHAT ARE YOU WAITING FOR!!!?" "GO AND BRING THAT!!!" Smira got teary eyes and said," i am sorry mother, please forgive me.." Her mother was fixed with her words. Smira now felt a little regret. She took slow steps towards the drawer where Scissors was lying.

The man,Uncle Liza got a call. He panicked.

He said,"you need to hurry! there is no time for this punishment we need to leave her right at this moment!" Her mother hold her hand so tightly and slapped her so hard, Her pink cheeks turned into red once again. It hurted her so much. She was racked with pain. It was the first time, her mother had slapped her two in a row. It was surely the most hurting punishment than those sevre punishments. Smira's tears came out. Although she was not her real mother as Smira thought, it hurted, Both mentally and physically.

Her mother asked her to get ready with her stuffs and to sit in the car hastily.

Smira went in her room and threw the pillow, a sign to show anger and grief. She cried in the bathroom. Quickly she started packing the stuff. She saw the phone, she was on the fence. She was having hard time whether to take it with her or to throw it.

BEEP BEEP

SMIRA!!!!!!! DO YOU WANT TO DIE??? COME FAST!!!!!

Smira quickly took the phone hide it in her bag and ran towards the car. It was the second time she sat in a car. The car started and so the new and fresh experience journey started. Smira was not at all aware where she was going, whether she will be safe there? whether she will enjoy? or she will be treated so severe than here. Whatever things will happen to her, she had made up her mind for them.

Her mother was giving her instrusctions. But she was not at all interested in hearing those rutheless commands. Because she knew, all the things are good and enjoyable were illegal for her. Instead of feeling bad and complaining about her luck, she happily looked out of the window, enjoying the stuffs. She was first time looking at the things with a close distance. She thought to open the car gate and run far away from her mother and lizard faced.

To enjoy her life like a normal one!

But she was not able to cross the trap. She was not scared and she did not have that much courage. This trap made a place in her life. Now she was developing the habit of being trapped.

While glancing the view of how world works, she saw John, She hid herself hiding the fact that she is hiding, from her mother. She bent down and did some stuff with her shoes. She was multitasking at that time. Checking that John has gone, Hiding this fact from her mother and keeping herslef calm.

Car stopped

"Why the car stopped?" her mother asked. It was like her mother gave words to her thoughts. Uncle Liza said,"Let me buy some cigars." Smira hoped that her mother will strictly deny, as the way they hurried, there was no time for this useless buyings."

"Buy one pack for me also."

"Whattt!!!?" Smira's thoughts. She eye rolled at them and said to her mind,"they are so noob criminals!"

She saw, John and Alice both were asking people something.

Smira was sweating out. Her legs were vibrating. She was sad because of loss of Ms. Amanda but the fact of the reaction Alice and John will give after hearing about Ms. Amanda scares Smira more.

Her head was down. John and Alice were two cars far from Smira.

Smira said,"I need to use the restroom!!!"

"No...you can't"

Smira said,"please mother!!!!"
Her mother sighed,"Come with me..."

They passed from Alice. Alice said," i..i.." John came and said,"what happened?"

Alice was doubtful. She said," that lady looked familiar."

John said,"don't waste time. We need to find our mother. Hope she is fine."

Smira's tear fell

She went in the rest room and waited her mother to go inside, after her mother went inside. She slowly locked the door from outside and came outside the restroom.

She saw it was a huge and luxurious mall.

Some highschool students were hanging out, One was sleeping on the chair, they took off their coat from face and jumped to stood up.

Smira was shocked, this incident was from her dream. She started looking at them.

That student had a baddy yet gorgeous look, their eyes were unbothered, personality was ten on ten. In highschool uniform they were slaying theirselves.

Smira got lost in enduring them. Totally forgot about her mother was locked.

IX

"WOW... a total mysterious person," Smira was lost in this thinking. That group of highschool passed from her, Smira turned back, she got surprised as she saw Alice and John coming. She quickly turned back and fell down as she hit herself from that mysterious person.

"sorry..." a cold voice came.

Smira did not even hesitate to ghost that person and she left quickly. That person thought,"what a mysterious girl."

Smira had a relaxed breathe, after she came at a certain distance from John and Alice. She looked around her, she enjoyed the view as it was her first time experiencing the environment of mall. Rich building, magical staircase, Enormous stalls of variety of items, floor so slippery as if it was just washed.

"What are you doing?" Smira looked back and she got startled. It was uncle Liza. Smira stuttered "i....i...." Uncle Liza was coming closer second by second, smira was walking backwards as his steps were getting closer. Smira felt confused, she looked at her right, she saw Alice and John were walking. She looked at her front, Uncle Liza was coming close. She was scared, but more than being scared she was confused.

"You look like a lizard.... sorry ugly lizard." A rude and cold voice came. Smira got hit from the owner of this voice. After getting hit by this voice, Smira had a vibe on which she could depend. As if it came purposely to rescue her from this scaringly confused situation. Smira looked back, A 6 feet tall lad, hands inside pants, wearing a school's uniform in ill mannerd way, buttons of shirt were open, a black t shirt was inside shool's shirt. Wearing aesthetic sneakers. It was the same high school lad, The mysterious one.

But this time, Smira could see in his eyes, they were bothering.

"What gibberish you are talking about?" angerness flowed out from Uncle Liza. The lad said,"you will answer...". Security blossomed and Smira felt hallowed and breezy. This was best feeling felt by Smira till now. The boy continued,"why are you harassing her?" Smira's eyes enlarged. For the first time someone took stand for her. She was having butterflies all over her body, goosebumps rose over her arms, this time these goosebumps rose because of lovely feeling she was having, with just a tiny act done by that boy.

The boy hold her hand and pulled her, Now Smira was behind him. In between Smira and lizard faced uncle stood the boy. Like a sheild, looking like as if the key to the impalpable trap was found.

Uncle Liza stuttered,"w..who are you ?" The boy said scratching his messy and uncontrollable hairs which lay themselves on his forehead, which could be barely be seen. "does it matter?" Uncle Liza laughed and then got angry. "She is my daughter!" Smira got surprised. The boy turned back and reassured it. Smira slowly and regretfully nodded. The boy looked up and laughed. "Now get out! you have got embarassed! leave father and daughter alone!" The boy swallowed and in a blink, he punched uncle Liza.

Smira was at highest level of shockness. The situation became warm and cool at the same time. Smira felt happy and relaxed after getting shocked.

why am i feeling different?

Why am i feeling so strong?

its a wierd feeling! is it because of this lad?

is he..... is he really my key for the trap?

can i trust him?

I feel so relaxed the moment he hold my hand, stood for me, and.... and..... he even punched that lizard...ugly lizard faced man!!

i....i..it feels like only he is the key!

While Smira was thinking her fairy tale thoughts and Uncle Liza was busy in covering his emabarass, Smira's mother was locked inside the restroom. Her anger is a top notch for creating a disaster. And at that moment his anger was at its peak. What will happen to Smira can not be predict. She shouted,"that punk! SMIRAAAAAAAAAAAAAAAAA!!!!" and pushed the door so hard that the door broke from the hinges. A lady washing her hands got a heart attack, after witnessing Smira's mother's act. Smira's mother was in extreme bad mood. Her face was haunting so badly.

Uncle Liza was about to slap the boy. Smira pulled the boy and ran with him, after reaching a little far, Smira said,"i...i...i..." Uncle Liza lost them, he banged his head.

Smira said,"i.....i...." The boy got annoyed and said,"you will take the whole day!" Smira made a poker face. And something strange hit her thoughts. She kept queit. The boy said,"who are you? and what you need from me?" Smira's heart broke.

Although it was not the boy's fault. It was all Smira's delusion.

Smira said in cracking voice,"then...then... why do you come and helped me?"

slowly her voice became a crying voice and she continued,

"helped me from that bastard? who is not my father! even that lady is not my mother!"

"why did you came?"

"why did you acted like you are my key? why!!?"

The boy was confused, he said,"if there would be aany other girl, getting harassed i would have done the same!!"

"why? are you the police?" Smira's expectations were on that boy.

"No... i am a human being! and it is important to do good deeds. Help the other person who are in trouble." The boy answered so reluctantly.

Till now Smira's tears were bursting out. The boy said,"cool down. That man will never harass you." "to be honest that man looks like a lizard." Smira in a crying voice said,"no..... he looks like an ugly lizard!" The boy laughed and Smira also laughed while crying.

They both sat. The boy offered some juice to her. It is wierd and strange but Smira was having juice for the first time!

Smira curiously asked," what is this..?" The boy was still, he said," do not joke around." Smira was serious and confused simultaneously. She said,"no..i am serious." The boy said,"Seriously? you haven't had this before?" Smira refused.

The boy told her about the juice, he felt strange. Smira said," you are not able to digest the fact that i do not know about a juice, you will be so shocked if i will tell you, i have never seen the world, and that its my first and maybe last time visiting place like this."

"I... I... feel so wierd thinking that i am in a trap. A trap where stepping outside the house is a crime, having phone is a disaster and disobeying the evil mother results in sevre punishments."

The boy was very confused,"are you from the fairy tale of cinderella? or are you....." Smira looked with sad eyes, "OHH.... YOU ARE PROMOTING YOUR FAIRY TALE."

"Fairy tale, the story is nice, i almost cried it's good. Although i am a bad boy in my school, but it was heart touching."

Smira looked at him and smiled.

no one will believe me...

no one will understand me...

i am born in this trap and i will die in this trap only

no key is there for this trap..

Because its an **IMPALPABLE TRAP.**

Smira said,"i thought you were the key of my trap."

The boy was confused. He doubted,"what trap?"

Smira said," let's see what destiny has poured for me."

"Smira... my dear.." Her barbaric and evil mother enterred the stage. Smira's heart started pounding. The boy greeted her mother. Smira was in a deep shock. She will face a lot sevre punishments. The boy said, "Hello.....haishh.. in our talks, i forgot to ask you your name..." "Smira..." Smira answered in a timid way. She was feeling very uncomfortable. The boy offered handshake saying,"hi Smira.. it was nice talking to you... myself Erick." Smira's mother rose her eyes seeing this act.

Smira's eyes were down, but in second by second she was looking up to check her mother. Her mother hold her hand and pulled her, pretending to be nice. Erick waved at her and was about to left the place. Smira quickly held his hand, Erick felt warmth, he looked at Smira. It was like she don't want to be with herpj mother, she was feeling insecure in front of her mother. Plus, Uncle Liza also enterred the stage.

Erick thought to stay.

Erick slowly asked,"what happened Smira?" Smira was shaking so badly.

Her mother took Erick with her, and Smira's hands fell hopelessly.

Uncle Liza said,"I told you...". Smira recalled her dream, the boy was killed by her mother. Smira's breathing stopped. She thought," i can not let this happen. I need to stop her." She Shouted,"ERICK!!!!" and fell down.

The world got mute, only she could listen was caring voice of Erick who came and lift her to the hospital. He sat outside the room, Smira's mother and uncle Liza were standing a little far. Uncle Liza asked,"what are you doing!!?" She smirked and went to Erick.

She said in a very evil tone, which Erick was not able to feel. "Smira..... she is a very sweet girl." Erick nodded.

"But.... unfortunately.. she...she...." She pretended crying, crocodiles tears came out from her evil eyes. "She is not normal...." Erick got shocked,"what do you mean by this?"

"Dear Erick... she makes people fool....no one dares to trust her."

She tells everyone that she is trapped by her mother! she is treated so badly and that her father is not her father." Erick was confused, he questioned,"You both are married?" "yes...its been so many years.But everytime his father tries to have a convo with her... she acts like he is harassing her."

Now, Erick was very much confused, He stood up and went inside the room. Smira said,"Erick..you are alright?"

she relaxed. Erick said,"i am alright! but you are not!"

"We met just now, a bond was created! but you broke it! i am going.. thankyou for making me fool!"

Smira cried,"do...don't go!! Erick please don't go!! if you will go they will kill me!! Erick..."

Erick got a headache he said,"they are your family!!!" and he left. Smira saw him leaving and darkness again covered her life. Big and fat drops of insecurity, trap and torture rolled over her crying face.

Her mother enterred, "my dear smira.... you have reached the limits! from where you got these gutts?"

Smira started shivering.

"see.. for the first time, you visited a mall, made a MALE friend, and now relaxing in the hospital!"

"Have you ever wondered why i treat you like a caged animal?"

Smira looked at her expecting some reason..

"I enjoy doing that!!" She laughed.

Smira was so helpless. Her mother said," i told you not to socialize! HAVEN'T I?" Smira nodded. "HOW DARE YOU DO THEN? HOW DARE YOU MAKE A FRIEND!? AND THAT ALSO A MALE!!!???"

"you know your punishment. right?" Smira sadly nodded.

The door of the room was closed and screaming of Smira were coming out of the room. It's not like no one could hear her screaming, no one was bothered to listen and help her.

The door opened, Smira's hairs were now short till her neck. Scars all over her hands and face. Maybe they were on her back, legs and everywhere. It was hospital, many tools were available. It's a real mystery from which tool her mother used.

As described earlier, her mother is an unexplainable lady. Poor Smira, had lost all her hopes and accepted her death in this trap.

She was alone in the room, it was her last day at the hospital.

no key is there!!!! no one will understand !!!!

i will surely die!!

Smira throwed pillow and complaint with anger, She cries while she is angry... She was having mental breakdown. Thinking of Erick!

X

"hello.....long time no see..."

"yeah... how are you doing?"

"fine...... but sometimes it's difficult to take care of kids, as i go to work.."

"oh.. it's a problem..dear..ohh..how about you leave your kids at daycare..?"

"i have tried.. but they.. they...don't like to socialize..."

"dear... it's a big problem, children need to socialize, or it will affect their future.

Socializing is the major part to be taught to our babies."

"hmm... you are right.. well how are your kids?"

"ohhh... Ramiya is now in highschool...."

Conversation on the phone call among two friends.

A cool mother sitting and eating her favourite snack while talking on the phone.

"maa... i have come!"

a tired voice came, it was a beautiful, pretty and bold highschool girl, just arrived from the school. Her mother continued,

"Ohhhh.... dear i got an amazing idea. You can leave your kids with Ramiya!" Ramiya's ears got active like a fox after hearing this statement. She came to her mother with half

tie opened, with muted voice she said,"never!!! why are you doing this." her eyebrows making a V.

Her mother did not even think before ignoring her.

Conversation on the phone continued,

"ommo....no...she have her studies to dealt with.."

"Naaaaa!! she is now on holiday, one month holiday.. you can send your kids till one month".

"aigu... it's so caring of you...thankyou so much!"

"gosh! no problem."

*phone hunged up**

Ramiya was still as if her whole life got ruined. She pulled her tie which was already half untied and throwed it. She turned to her mother and shouted.

"maaa!! how can you do this!!!???"

"i was so excited for these holidays!!!"

Her mother gave a reluctant reply while putting the empty plate of her favorite snack, she just ate. "really? what things makes these holidays excited? my madame?"

Ramiya said in a helpless voice,"i..i....i..." she had no answer to the question asked.

Her mother smiled and came to her, squished her cheeks. Ramiya said,"don't do that! i am a grown up now!" Her mother replied,"ohhh it's a serious problem ....." She hugged her and cuddled up saying,"my little princess is a grown up now!!!". While Ramiya laughed and giggled saying,"Maa...don't do it."

After the cute act of mother and daughter, Ramiya layed down such a way that her head was on her mother's lap.

Her mother started playing with her not so long hairs, and said "look Ramiya... i know you have your own life, and you like doing things for your own. But my dear, those kids need to be taught to socialize, just like i taught you when you were young!"

Ramiya listened carefully to her mother. Ramiya is a very understanding personality, knows how to dealt with problem. When she was 8, her father died. Since then her mother is the only one whom she is close with. Ramiya do not have any true friends, whole class loves to talk with her, but she could not find a true friend.

But her mother, never let her feel alienated. She could share everything with her mother and her mother would direct her the right path. This lead in building up trust towards her mother. Her mother was an ideal one i must say.

Her mother continued," some kids are trapped with anti social cage. Promise me, if you ever find anyone like that, you will help them!"

Ramiya stood up and nodded.

she was looking in her mother's eyes,

her mother felt a little concious and said,"what's this staring for?"

Ramiya laughed and said,"it's not staring! it's a reaction after realizing that how precious you are! my beautiful and best mother!"

Her mother laughed and said." gosh!! stop being so cheezy " Ramiya laughed back. Her mother pat her back saying, "get up!! wash your face and get ready."

Ramiya stood up and took an apple from fruit basket. The fruit basket was very antique and it's beauty was getting old day by day. It was given by her mother's grandparents. Her maternal and paternal sides were very conservative.

Their thoughts were very typical. But her mother was different from everyone in there family, instead of strictly saying NO or scolding, she handles the situation or a problem calmly, she understands every phase of life, how a teenager thinks, she was aware about what changes occurs in the teenage years.

This is the reason Ramiya felt so comfortable and secured with her mother, that she shares even a minute detail of her life with her mother,unlike the other teenagers, who mostly keeps secret from their parents which leads to a distance between the parents and their children.

And unlike other parents, who first see soceity and then at their children, who reacts so harshly to any problem created by their children, instead of giving priorty to making their kids relaxed they give priorty to scold them, Her mother simply gives a nice warm hug and suggests her what she should do?

One day, The fault was of Ramiya, She took a pen of her friend without her permission, Her mother did not scold her and told her in an immature way, so that it does not look like she was ordering Ramiya,

The next day, Ramiya apologised and gave the pen back.

Her way of parenting was not appreciated by either of the sides, This created a wall of hatred between her and them, that fruit basket have all those memories, everytime she looks at the basket, The movie of the past plays in her mind.

Ramiya took a bite of crunchy and watery apple, chewed it and said,"who is coming?"

Her mother said,"Erick! your childhood friend....remember?"

Ramiya felt very embarassed.

Her mother layghed and teased her," when he came here last time, you were in kindergarten... and you....."

"Mother!!!!" Ramiya irritatingly interrupted.

her mother laughed even more.

Ramiya's face was all covered with embarassment.

She recalled,

when she was young, she used to play with Erick. They were pretty close.

When it was Erick's last visit, Her heart was broken

They both were sitting and playing, Erick said,"let's play in the park.."

they ran towards the park, Ramiya said,"hey! push me". Ramiya sat on the swing and Erick pushed her.

It was Ramiya's turn to push, without asking him she pushed him so hard, That he made a parabola before felling down.

Ramiya did not even looked at his state, she ran and locked herself in the door.

"Ramiya!!Ramiya!! Erick is leaving! it's his last meeting!"

Ramiya closed her ears with the pillow.

She came back to the present and said,"maaa!! why is he coming?"

Her mother said,"he will live on rent in neighbourhood."

"AGAIN!!!!?"

Her mother banged Ramiya's head and said,"hmmm!"

"go get ready!!fast!"

Ramiya went to her room.

She relaxed on her bed, and looked at the window, the whether was very pleasant.

She smiled and said,"why would be anyone trapped..?"

"It is a free world!"

Suddenly, the thoughts of Erick invaded her overthinking mind. Her face was so covered with embarassment,"how will i face him!!!?" "uhhhh". She wiggled up and curled on her bed. A wave of second thought came. Her facial expressions changed up and she said,"so what!!?? i was 5 years old!" "he would have forgotten all those stuff!"

She sat straight convincing herself, But instead she was getting confused and confused.

"RAMIYA!!!RAMIYA!!!COME DOWNSTAIRS!!LOOK WHO IS HERE!"

Ramiya freezed,and said,"gone!"

She took breathes and calmed herself.

She came downstairs, her eyes were looking at the floor. As she arrived beside her mother, She looked up.

Her cute bunny eyes met those unbothered foxy eyes. She said,"E..Erick?" Erick nodded and smiled.

Ramiya said,"you have changed so much!" Erick said,"but you did not!" Ramiya got confused.

"You are still so stubborn and ugly!". Ramiya got angry and ran behind him to beat him.

Their mother laughed.

Ramiya and Erick had fun after so many years, their day was spent in their frivollous rebukes, nostalgia covered their bodies. Ramiya was very delighted.

They both sat outside the house.

Erick said,"so....any updates?" Ramiya looked at him and said,"Not that much serious! you speak!"

Erick thought to tell Smira's stuff.

he said,"Yesterday, i met a girl...she was good....but...."

Ramiya asked,"but......" Erick continued "She was mentally ill... but i am so confused, she did not looked like one! She was telling me...she is in a trap!!! and that i am her key..."

"i am confused!"

Ramiya pat her back and said,"who told you she is mentally ill...?"

"her own mother!"

Ramiya said,"today.. my mother told me..their are people who are trapped and we need to help them..you should have helped her!"

Erick felt regret.. He said,"bro! this house is scary! who lives their?"

Ramiya said,"it's a haunted house! an old couple lives here"

Ramiya realised something and jumped,"shit! tomorrow is the day!!!! every sunday, A meal is cooked for them by my mother!!! and i need to go there!"

Erick laughed and said,"all the best!"

he hit her back and ran away.

Ramiya shouted,"you!!!! you will come with me tomorrow!!!!"

She went inside her house and said,"that annoying brat!!"

Her mother poured milk and gave it to Ramiya saying,"what happened? your embarassment turned into anger?"

Ramiya took a sip and said,"embarasment!!! my foot!! he is so annoying!" Her mother said,"well....you would be absolutely right...but there is no need to use that kind of words..my dear!!"

Ramiya realised and said,"sorry...."

Her mother said,"Ramiya....tomorrow a guest will come at your grandpa and grandma's house!" She was talking about her paternal grandparents. Ramiya said,"Mother!! i hate them!! they disowned this title! the moment they throwed you out!"

"And that guest would also be like them only!!! selfish and rude!"

She went in her room, she did not gave a little chance for her mother to speak.

Her mother took the empty glass and washed it. She sat on the sofa and had a deep sighed.

"something's not right! the guest.... the guests!! i feel bad about them!"

She said, as if she was worried.

XI

Oxymoron environment spread out, the morning was pleasant but cruel. A not so good 4 wheel vehicle moving slowly. A deep and intense environment's creation held there. Now, Smira was not allowed to even look out of the window, She was forced to set herself in the boot of the white and scratched car. Smira set herself with uncomfortability, there was no option to look outside, what is going in the world..

Dirty floor of the car's part was grossing out. Smira was scared but had accepted that there is no key for her trap. She is living in that trap for so long that now, she has developed its adaptation, although she fears out whenever she sees her mother.

why is it so?

what she wants?

she do not want me to go anywhere far from her... yet she treats me like a hostage.. uh..worse than a hostage!

where are we going?

will i be more trapped?

or

will i be able to explore the world...

Smira's eyebrows squished, as if they tried to meet, but forehead make walls, folds of skin between them, as she thought.

Here, we are here!!

uncle Liza shouted with a state of being relaxed and excited at the same time, her mother smirked and looked at the building as well as locality.

Uncle Liza got out of the car, and spread his arms in the air as if a hard task was over.

The door of the car's part opened where Smira folded herself. A ray of light sparkled on Smira's eyes, As the light faded, a face was getting more clear. It was not the face, Smira had seen before..

A very new face to her, but she felt somehow relaxed after having a glance of that face.

"Ramiya! come here!" an ordering voice struck the environment. But this voice was not ordering at all for Smira!

She had expirienced the ordering voice of her mother, it was a very big difference in both ordering voices.

Ramiya stood still, figuring out who came as a "guest" at her so called grandparents house. Shrinking her eyes, folding her arms and analysing the scene in front of her.

Smira's mother got down and said,"come out fast!"

Ramiya was surprised, the way of talking was not very nice, even to speak to your daughter, this was a harsh and a very rude way of communicating.

Smira got out. She was unable to stand as she folded up herself for a little long time period. Ramiya was now very curious about Smira, Her eyes could clearly tell what she was thinking...

who are they?

who is this girl?

is this a way to talk to daughters or sons?
something's wrong with them!
i need to figure out!

Ramiya's mother came outside the house and gave her a packat, the packat was covered with beautiful cloth and a soothing smell of food rose from it. She stopped her act as she got distracted by the scene in front of her, she looked at Smira. Smira looked at them. Ramiya was busy in her deep thoughts while her mother smiled at Smira.

Smira looked at her, She waved at Smira with a raise in her eyes. Smira was a lot surprised, she thought..

woa... is she that girl's mother?
she is an angel!!!
she has allowed her daughter to step outside
and her smile.... it is so comfortable!!

but Smira had not a single expression on her face, Smira's mother held her arm and pulled her, it was looking very cruel, those pointed and evl fingers pierced on Smira's thin and white arms, but Smira was used to it, so she was not scared or stressed.

They enterred the house, That haunted house.

It was named as a haunted house by Ramiya, as the elevation of the house was just like a rotten house in old movies, Green patches of cyanobacteria covered the walls of the house, Two storeyed house, windows were broken, The curtains torned out, and there lived an old couple, Ramiya's grandparents.

They have liked the house the way it is. After the death of Ramiya's father, His father'S family showed their true colours to her mother, they started torturing her and one day they throwed her out of the house. After a lot struggle and hard work, her mother got successful and financially stable. The only reason she bought a house near Ramiya's grandparents's one was,

After Ramiya's mother was thrown out, gradually the family members started withering. Maybe we can call this *karma*. Grandparents left alone, everybody left them alone in that house, the house where their childhood lies, the house where frivolous rebukes lies were now abandon by themselves only, it hurted them a lot.

Ramiya's mother took care of them, she performs her duty so well, although she is not allowed in that house, but from neighbour she keeps eye on them.

That is why, she got to know taht some guests are arriving at their place.

The broken door opened with a cracky voice and an old man came out holding a stick for support, wrinkles on his face, yet he looked so strict, his physique was just like that of an army man. Ramiya's mother was still, she had seen him this close after the decades.

Ramiya's mother somehow felt delighted, she recalled Ramiya's father in that old men.

Then a beautiful, old lady followed him, Her back was bent, and less wrinkles were there on her white and spotless face, she wore an old set of clothes, It was clear that they both lived alone, no one was there to take care of them.

Ramiya's mother smiled seeing both of them.

Ramiya looked at them and said through gritted teeth, "look...look at them.. living their life as if they are proud what they have done! i hate everyone in that house! and these two guests sucks!!"

A hard slap hit Ramiya on her back.

Ramiya glanced back, it was Erick.

Ramiya said in anger, frustration could be clearly seen in her voice,"get lost! i am very angry already!"

Erick shrugged, and said,"why is it so!?"

Ramiya pointed towards her grand parents.

But Erick's eyes met Smira.

Erick's abnigation could be seen, His eyes rose and her legs struck.

His mouth automatically said,"SMIRA!?"

Ramiya looked at him confusingly.

She said,"do you know her?"

Erick took so long to process, Smira's presence was dubious for him.

Ramiya clicked her fingers in front of his unbothered eyes, the eyes which were processing,

Erick came in his senses and said,"I..I.. have met her before.."

"she is the one whom i was talking about.. but how is she her? she was in the hospital...and the doctor had intstructed her, to remain admitted for 4 to5 days, why is she her..?"

Ramiya was very confused, what a mysterious thing came in front of her.

She got determined.. that she will solve the mystery of Smira.

The grandparents, were not happy with their guests.

The only thing forced them to get agree, was money.

Uncle Liza and Smira's mother enterred the house, and Smira tagged along.

Smira was neither happy, nor sad

neither excited nor scared.

neither nervous nor confused.

Till now she got pro in accepting the baddest of all situations also.

They all sat on the broken sofa, springs came out, and covers, torned out.

Uncle Liza started the conversation...

"ummm well...this is our little Smira...she will be living here, now we are getting late...we will leave now.. your money has been transferred."

That old couple nodded.

Uncle Liza and her mother left, Before leaving her mother came to Smira and warned her. Usually, mothers or any other, while leaving say something like,*i will miss you*

take care

we will meet again!

but instead she said,"mind yourself! and if my parenting gets affected, i will kill you!"

she kissed her forehead and left.

Smira did not react. She stood still and saw the car getting smaller and smaller, as they went far and far.

After they left, Smira came inside.

That old couple said,"see.. it's been a long time, we have cared for anyone.

"there is a lady in our neighbour, she will send you your food stuffs."

Smira nodded with eyes down in respect.

They continued," you can do whatever you want..just do not bother us!"

Smira's eyes got so big, as if they will come out if she opened it a little bit more.

Smira's life blossomed again.

she stutterd,"wh...what..whatever i want?"

"yes.... but it should not affect our payment and our personal life!"

Smira was so happy that she lost her control and hugged them.

That made goosebumps all over their body. They looked at each other, and rememberred their kids. their young times.

An emotional environment hit them both, they were about to get melt.

Instead they controlled themselves and pat Smira's back and said,"ok ok...now do not disturb us! get lost!"

Smira was very happy, for the short period, forlorn turned into it's opposite, although she was still lonely, but she was not caged.

She ran outside and felt those fresh air! cherished the beauty of nature and played along with the animals and insects, in those ten minutes she had explored enough.

"what's your name?" Smira looked back, Ramiya was standing folding her hands. Ramiya knew her name, She wanted to start their conversation.

Smira's eyes pulled down, as if she was shy and scared.

Ramiya sat beside her, and said,"common!! am i an evil monster!?"

Smira's trust on friendship and making friends was shattered.

she kept quiet.

Ramiya offered her a nice and friendly handshake.

Smira could not resist any longer, she accepted the handshake.

Ramiya smiled

Smira looked at her and smiled.

Ramiya shouted,"OMMO!!"

Smira got shocked,"wh..what happened?"

Ramiya said,"YOU...YOU.... HAVE DIMPLES!!!"

Smira blushed,

She said,"really....do i..?"

Ramiya took out her phone and opened camera.

Ramiya said,"smileeeee!"

Smira was shy, she did not smiled."

Ramiya got annoyed.

She got an idea.

She hold the phone from one hand, and from the other hand, she tinkled Smira.

That was a beautiful natural laugh of Smira.

Having so cute dimples, her lips making an ideal shape and her white perfect teeth, rabbit teeths, made her look so beautiful. Smira had never laughed before, it was the first time for her as well to know, she had dimples and a very cute smile. Ramiya stored that beautiful smile in her phone.

Erick saw them.

He looked at Smira laughing with those beautiful dimples she had, but never showed to anyone.

Erick went their and said,"hi...girls.."

As Smira looked at him, she got angry.

She suddenly stood up and went inside the house.

Ramiya slapped his back and said,"you are a troublemaker till now!"

Erick was confused.

"Is she angry? from me?"

XII

Ramiya was wandering here and there, as if her problem's solution will pop out, if she will wander.

"how should i get close to her?

how can i find out.who she really is?

urgggg this problem is killing me!"

Her mother found out her struggling, she came and pretended to find something.

Ramiya noticed her mother,

"maa...what are you searching?"

"your brain!"

Her mother said, while hitting her head not so hard.

It was a joke, enough to make her smile. But this time, she did not smiled.

She was busy thinking a way.

Her mother sighed and sat on the sofa saying,"was my joke that bad!?"

Ramiya shook her head as if removing a cloud of thought surrounding her. And sat beside her mother.

"maa... what was the meaning of your joke!?"

Her mother gritted her teeth and said,"dumbo!!! how many times i have told you!! if you have any problem! mark this word any problem!!! there is only one single solution!

and that is come to me! share your problem with me!"

Ramiya looked down and nodded.

Her mother rubbed her soft cheeks and said,"tell me.... why my little girls is tensed?"

Ramiya was confused, how to put on the words..?

She started,"the guest....the guest which came in our neighbour...i suspect..them."

Her mother was carefully listening to her.

"that man and that lady...they treated Smira rudely..i want to know.. Smira!"

Her mother gave a sad yet proud smile to her.

"Ramiya...you...have made me proud my dear..."

"but...we do not know..the truth.."

"exactly.. i need to find that truth mother!!" Ramiya said, interrupting her mother's speech.

Her mother did not felt right about it. She said,"ok....go for it..but in limits..it should not affect you! That girl... me...your grandparents.."

"Maaaa... why do you care about those people! they have kicked you out of your house!"

Ramiya's voice was clearly angry. She does not like her mother caring about her grandparents.

Her mother scolded her, but it did not felt like that. She is the sweetest and ideal person.

"you should not say rubbish about them dear, They are your grandparents."

"i know... but they do not deserve respect!"

Her mother was confused, Confused about how would she convince Ramiya.

After a tense face she become relaxed, and gave a fake smile.

She patted Ramiya's back and asked her to go in the room, as if she was not able to convince her at that moment.

She sighed and sat on the sofa, thinking what to do.

&

In the morning,
sunlight of peace shone on that cute face of Smira, Her eyes flinched inside those eyelids having big and dense eyelashes.

She opened the shatter of vision and looked outside the window, She stretched herself and looked outside.

Her eyes got bigger, when she saw Erick playing with a puppy.

His voice was quite loud to be heard by Smira.

"Barb! come catch it!"

The little piece of cotton ran here and there.

Erick glanced up at Smira, and his eyes stopped.

Smira felt awkward, she was not able to express herself.

Erick waved his hand and said,"hey!"

Smira bit her lips and waved back looking down. She was not aware of the time, when she started talking to him.

Erick actioned her to come down.

Poor Smira's habit of being trapped came in front of her and she denied.

"SMIRA!SMIRA!"

The old lady called her with a cracking voice,

Smira quickly went to them, leaving Erick alone with the white puppy.

Smira saw the old woman decoratig the dining table with a variety of food stuffs.

Those boiled eggs, baked bread and that cute circled pancakes and waffles from which chocolate rolled down and those fruits, which Smira have not even seen once in her life looked so cherishing to her, she dropped a drop of tear from eyes instead of dropping water from mouth.

That dining table was used after a lot decades, Last time it was used was when Ramiya's father arrived home after a tiring day and brought snacks on the way, whole family sat together and had dinner.

Smira stopped the old lady,"granny...do not do it...you sit here, i will do! grandpa come fast!"

The old lady was moved by this word, she sat with a jerk and goosebumps rose all over her arms.

Smira did all the chores like a pro, she even washed the dirty pile of dishes.

The old lady encountered her, she said,"why did you washed the dishes?"

Smira smiled and said,"because i love to wash the dishes."

"lier!"

"no ones love to wash the dishes!"

Smira held her hands, she felt her hands so soft as if a little harder touch will destroy them, Smira said,"granny... thankyou..."

The old woman was feeling very good but she did not expressed it.

her voice cracked,"see....do not say this word again!"

"why?....."

it was almost two weeks, since Smira's mother left her.

And she created a nice bond with the old couple,

they were not that rude and cruel from inside as they pretend to be one of them...

and Smira starting loving them as if they are her real granny and grandpa.

XIII

"Erick!!! suggest me an idea please!"

Erick was confused and speechless in front of Ramiya's problem.

Erick tried to convince her

"Ramiya.. you are overthinking!"

"OVERTHINKING! what! Erick!?" Ramiya's voice got angry.

Erick continued,"see.... i have seen Smira and her family. Her mother loves her! and how can a mother be so cruel to her own daughter!?"

Ramiya shouted,"Erick!!! you are just denying it! you have also seen, the act of her mother! There is something...something mysterious about that family!"

Erick calmed himself and said slowly,"are you stressed about your grandparents? that they will be in a trouble?"

Ramiya paused for a second and said,"why there topic came in front? huh? i am talking about that girl! and listen to me very carefully! they both do not belong to me! whether they live or die! it does not matter to me at all!"

Erick spoke in a high tone,"Accept it! you care about them! still!" and left.

Ramiya could not speak anything after that.

She stood confused.

The evening was heavy, it was unusual.

Ramiya went outside and looked at the sky, sky was behaving abnormal as if something strange is happening.

while enduring and analysing the weather and the situations, her eyes met Smira.

Smira was on the balcony looking at Ramiya. Ramiya waved at her and asked to join her.

Smira smiled

Ramiya shouted, "are you free right now!?"

Smira paused for a second to analyse the sentance and then said in confusion,"me.....? right now....?"

Ramiya raised her brows and said,"yes...you....darling...." and gave a warm and a smile whom she could trust and rely on.

Smira could not resist the beautiful ear to ear smile on her face. She said,"I...I.. "

Ramiya said,"Well i guess we do not have the whole day girl!" Smira interrupted," No.. wait..." She wore her shoes and ran down the stairs. Ramiya laughed.

Smira reached the garden and saw Ramiya waiting for her.

Ramiya asked,"what took you so long! don't you like me..?"

Smira did not took a sec in answering,"No.. it's not like that....." Smira looked here and there as if she was searching someone. Ramiya encountered her act and asked," what happened? looking for someone?"

Smira said," umm.... Erick......?"

Ramiya laughed and said," ughh... Girl... do you hate me..?" Smira hesitated,"I..I.. am not comfortable with him......"

Ramiya looked in her eyes, while Smira's eyes were continously staring the grass.

Ramiya thought something, and came up with the idea.

Ramiya took Smira's hand and ran. Smira could not analyse until they reached bus stop....

Smira stressed out and got anxious. She was shivering as if she was possessed.

Ramiya couldn't think of something good.. but she quickly hugged Smira. For the first time, Smira had experienced such a warm and peaceful thing. Her shivering body relaxed, she went in a full peace zone.

Ramiya said,"girl...it's alright..."

Smira took deep breathes and after getting completely calm her voice whispered,"my mother will kill me if she finds out..."

Ramiya said,"And what if she doesn't?"

Smira looked at Ramiya.

Ramiya's loyal black eyes winked.

They both sat in the bus.

with the start of bus's engine, start of enjoyment in Smira's life could be seen.

but that little human was not enjoying, maybe... she had never known how to enjoy things. Ramiya looked at her. Smira was looking down.

Ramiya said,"here....let's switch seats."

Smira sat near the window. Winds of freedom hugged her, her hairs flew with confidence and an automatic beautiful smile appeared on her face.

Ramiya smiled, " ommo... look Smira have dimples....!"

Smira got confused and stopped smiling.

Ramiya said,"girl..... you look damn pretty when you smile... why don't you smile?" Smira asked in a low voice.." what's dimple?" Ramiya sighed and shouted,"you gotta kidding me!"

Smira didn't understand.

Ramiya said,"wait.."

she took out her phone and opened camera, and said " on the count of 3"

"3...2...1.... smileeee"

they took selfies

This boosted Smira's confidence.

Ramiya said,"so....where do you want to go first..?"

Smira was blank.

Ramiya said,"ummmm..... ferris wheel..?"

Smira nodded.

Ramiya said,"alright.. lets goooo"

Before enetring the amusement park, she called her mother.

"*"hello......?"*

hello maa.... i am at amusement park...
"Ummm... well what time will you be back...?"
I will be back before 6 PM
"Ok... honey...take care"
mumma.... i am with Smira....
"Smira.......?"
Yes..."

her mother analysed and took a deep sigh...

"*"alright.. but take care of her too..."*

yes sure mumma...
"that's good that you informed... but you need to take care....."
"should i send Erick too..?"
No...No... no need... trust your daughter

"i do... darling.... come home safe.. bye..."
bye maa...love you..
"love you too hun..."

Ramiya put her phone inside...

Smira said,"you got a nice mother..."

Ramiya laughed,"what...?"

Smira said," no.. i mean.. she allows you to go here and there...."

Ramiya said,"it's because she trusts me....your mother do not trust you...?"

Smira sighed.

"i don't know whether she trusts me or not...she is different..."

Ramiya could clearly see, what Smira was trying to hide..

Instead of hearing the truth, Ramiya chose to make Smira enjoy.

They sat on the ferris wheel.. Ramiya was scared to death.

Smira was surprisingly enjoying the ride. Her dimples never fade once in the amusement park.

They both were having brunch now...

"i always wanted to spend a day like this.. thankyou Ramiya..."

"Gosh! you sound so formal!!!" said Ramiya."We are friends.... girlll!!!"

Smira smiled...

Ramiya did so...

"Ummmm.... You and Erick had a fight?"

Ramiya was surprised.

"how do you know..?"

Smira said," i came in the morning to give pancakes.. made by granny.."

Ramiya's soul flew and came back.

"how could that woman.... send something to us..... it is impossible... h..howw......"

"That woman..?" Smira whispered.

Ramiya tried to swallow this sentance and said,"i mean... granny... why would she give something to us..?"

Smira said,"You are her grand daughter....right..?"

Ramiya nodded.

Smira said,"She is not that bad.. infact they both want everyone's good. They both are just lonely...They need the lively house, they need someone whom they can scold, they need someone who can scold them. They want to enjoy the phase of grandparents.. They are good creatures.. Do not misunderstand them."

Ramiya listended calmly.

Smira smiled,"this is what i observed by living with them."

Ramiya changed the topic.

"in which school do you study..?"

Smira's smile went off.

Ramiya was confused. Smira said,"i had home schooling for 10years"

"i did got a chance to go to school.. but my mother didn't like friends stuff..so she again resumed my home schooling."

"But fees was too much... so home schooling also stopped."

Ramiya was still.

"Smira! is that you! gosh!!" a voice, a helpless voice struck their ears.

Smira looked back.

It was Alice.

Smira's heart skipped a beat.

Ramiya was confused.

Smira didn't look in Alice's eyes.

Alice said,"Smira! i need to know! only you can help us! please! try to understand!"

Ramiya looked at Smira.

Smira was looking the ground. She knew the whole truth but she was denying that she knew.

Ramiya said,"hello.. I am Ramiya... what's the matter..?"

Alice looked at Ramiya, tears overflew from her eyes.

Smira couldn't handle the situation. She stood up and said," i don't know!"

and ran.

Alice fell on knees and cried.

Ramiya made her stand and offer water to her.

Ramiya said,"i promise... you will get to know the truth."

Alice took a sip. Ramiya pat her shoulder and left.

Smira was walking the cold winds were making it more difficult for the tears to come out.

"Are you going to act like coward forever!?" shouted Ramiya.

Smira did not stopped.

"Answer me Smira! how could you be this coward! that you cannot help a daughter to find her mother!"

Smira did not stopped.. Her legs were walking and walking.

And here comes the shower from clouds.

"Don't you know! the realtion of a mother and a daughter!!"

Smira's leg stopped, unexpected. water drool over her body, and tears get lost with the drops of rain.

She turned back, Ramiya also stopped.

"YES! I DO NOT KNOW! WHAT IS A MOTHER DAUGHTER RELATION!"

"YES! I AM A HEARTLESS CREATURE!"

"HOW COULD I KNOW THE LOVE OF A DAUGHTER TO HER MOTHER OR A LOVE OF A MOTHER TO HER DAUGHTER! WHEN I HAVE NEVER EXPERIENCED THIS DAMN THING! RAMIYA! HOW COULD I!!!?

Smira was crying badly her heart ache.

Ramiya was still.

Smira continued,

"In these 14 years! i have never felt what love's feel like! i have never experienced the importance of mother or a father.. i have always wanted to escape from these creatures my entire life!"

"I do not understand! why we love them when all they do is trap you ! and what's the best part! nobody knows that you are trapped! it's you and only you! alone! crying for the freedom!"

"Yes! i have never loved my mother! you know why!? because she never loved me! never cared for me! all she did was torture, she tortured me day and night! and that's what made me hate this relation of parents!"

That was too much for Ramiya to swallow. And it was deadly painful for Smira to experience this her entire life.

 XIV

Ramiya hugged Smira. They both were all wet, Smira could not stop, she started crying but tears faded in rain. Ramiya said," you are stupid!!"

"Why haven't you shared this big hurting past of yours!?"

Smira wiped her tears and said," My mother is not My actual mother."

This was a big jerk for Ramiya. She said,"After knowing that she is not your real mother... you did not took any action?"

Smira laughed sarcastically.

"What can i even do? I am just a helpless girl, she never allowed me to do anything, i even have no phone or any other games to play, never played with neighbours or friends."

Ramiya was listening silently.

She said," Do not worry! I am with you Smira! I will find your real mother!"

"I WILL FIND THE KEY FOR YOUR IMPALPABLE TRAP"

Smira was still.

Her ears longed so much to hear this statement.

It felt so calm and melodious,

All Smira could do was, to say "thankyou".

Ramiya took her at her home. And offered Hot Chocolate milk to her.

Ramiya said," Can you please tell what happened to the girl's mother whom we met today?"

Smira was a bit nervous but she took a deep breathe and said," Her Mother is DEAD"

Ramiya was shocked.

She stuttered,"h...h..how?"

Smira took a minute to have gutts and then she told each and everything to Ramiya.

THUDDDD

"What in the world you both are talking about?" a confused and husky voice came.

Ramiya and Smira turned behind, Smira face was blue in shock.

Erick stood still in his gorgeous jersey his hairs all set just too perfect to be a hot sporty lad. His cold eyes were now raised as if he was having polyemotions.

Ramiya's eyes saw the football which had a nice fall a minute ago while Smira's were pinned towards Erick's which were doing the same.

After a moment of noisy silence,

Erick picked up his football which was brand new as if just bought, and he looked at the girls.

Smira moved her eyes from him this gave him a kind of sadness.

Smira stood up and passed through Erick like a soft wind, which Erick wished to hold but a part of him resist. Ramiya too stood up.

Erick wanted to say a lot.

But his mouth could only afford a calm and guilt 'sorry'.

Ramiya turned back and shouted," i told you Erick!!!" she slowly calmed her voice with a breathe and applied tripple 'c' method {being cool, calm and collected}

which she had learned in one of the twisted series by Ana Huang.

Erick said," i can not believe that all this shit is real!"

Ramiya said," its very hard to accept it as a truth! to accept that a mother can trap her child! but do you know Smira is living a life which she definitely do not deserves! that innocent creature haven't even laughed properly! everytime she have this fear, 'what will happen if mother sees me'!'

Ramiya pulled her hair lock beside her ears and said," Erick you should sincerely apologise to Smira." she left.

But before she could pass the door, Erick confirmed,"A mother can not do this to her daughter!"

Ramiya stopped.

"You're right...... she isn't her mother."

Ramiya left.

Erick banged the table beside him.

৩

Smira enterred the house, Grandma welcomed her with a glass of water.

Smira stopped. She was confused.

Grandma said,"Drink it or you will get dehyderated."

"Dehyderated?" Smira's question was dumb according to the age she was.

Grandma said,"Dehyderation comes when we do not drink enough water, we starts feeling dizzy." She took the glass after Smira poured the water in her stomach.

Smira had a fake smile and garnished it with a 'thankyou'.

Smira enterred her room and started crying.

Why am i crying!! i have not done anything wrong!! so whyyyy whyyyy whyyy!!

"Because you have a pure heart sweetheart." it was a voice from an old but it was filled with so care. Smira looked back,"oh.. grandma.."

she wiped her tears and stood up.

Grandma came to her and sat on the bed and actioned Smira to come close to her.

Smira was still.

Her heart made her do as directed without thinking any possibilities.

She sat beside her, a warm and caring vibe hugged Smira.

Grandma said,"Sometimes it is very hard to react to the things, you have been alone for so long... you have never been taught how to solve a social issue.. what are different menance which could jumpscare you on each step of your life."

Smira listened carefully.

Grandma continued...

"But don't worry pookie... you will figure it out.."

Smira did not realised when her head was now in grandma's weak laps and grandmas wrinkled hands started bearing her innocent head.

"because now you are not alone....."

Smira said,"No grandma i will be alone forever... Once Erick gave me a relaxation that i will get out of the trap but he too ditched my feelings... Ramiya will do the same... and once my mother comes you and grandpa will do the same. I was forever alone!"

Grandma got silent.

She wanted to hug Smira and never let her go with her monster mother.. But she did not.. Instead she sighed.

"Girl.... you are so young to have this judgement. Do you know which is the strongest thing human can do?"

"cry..?"

"You silly girl!" Grandma pat her head on her silly response. Which made Smira laughed.

Grandma continued,

"It's Hope. Me and your Grandpa have lived our whole lives on Hopes. Our marriage was succesful because of hopes, we fought every problem and situation with hopes. See we were lonely but we had hopes dear. So never ever lose hopes."

Smira said,"Now you are not lonely?" Grandma laughed.

"No dear.. Because we got you. Since you come in our dark house, each and every room of this house and our hearts, lighted up." Smira got silent.

After a while she said," What if mother came and she took me with her?" Grandma sighed," We will see things at that time.. Let's just enjoy the present...no..?" Smira had a deep,"hmmm".

Grandma ended her speech..

"So my little Smira.... what things you learned today???"

"First, Do not ever think you are lonely. Second, Always have hopes. Third, enjoy the present!"

Good girl... now i will not take more time on lecturing you.. or you will say," ughh what a boring granny!" Grandma had a sarcastic laugh. Which made Smira laugh too.

Smira slowly stood up and said," Grandma... i am so gratefull that you are with me! i have never got this sweetest and warmest lecture!" she hugged Grandma which made tears fell from her old eyes. Grandma had a hug after a decade in her life.

Before Smira got back in her position, Grandma wiped her tears.

Smira said," grandma... what does pookie means?"

"It's just a term of endearment used to describe something cute." Husky voice interrupted the conversation.

Smira looked behind, and found Erick dribbling his basketball.

He said," hey granny!!" Grandma said," Erick... how have you been?" Smira looked at the floor.

Erick said," I came here to apologise to your 'pookie'."

Grandma laughed and beat the air.

"you sarcastic lad!"

Grandma stood up and said,"dare you made Smira cry!"

Erick had a cute yet made up smile, he assured grandma with a kiss on her forehead."

Smira was sitting on the bed and still watching the pattern of the floor.

Erick sighed.

"Smira....."

Smira did not listened..

Erick said," are you ghosting me!!"

Smira did not responded.

Erick shouted in a low volume," YOU! GRANNY'S POOKIE!!!"

Smira had a laugh on her face but she hid it.

Erick said," ok.. so i need to do take over the PLAN B"

Smira looked at him.

He said," do you know.... how to run?"

Smira was too late to analyse the sentance.

SPLASH!

Erick threw water on her.. Poor Smira , her short hairs were all wet and water was dripping from her white face.

She shouted," Grandma!!!!!"

Erick said," catch me if you can!!!"

And he ran.. Smira had no choice she chased him.

XV

Erick went outside of the house. Smira was looking for grandma which automatically led her to the garden.

As she stepped on the green grass of the garden, A splash of water encountered her. It was then when she saw Ramiya and Erick, all wet. Water dripping from their clothes and face.

Erick's hair,messed up looking like a model of a magazine. Ramiya's face was full of joy.

Smira asked,"what are you both doing?"

Ramiya threw a water balloon and said,"water fight girll!!"

Smira turned back.

Ramiya and Erick stood confused," she did not liked it!" " i told you it was a bad idea!"

Smira picked two balloons ,one in each hand secretly and in a blink of an eye, both the balloon burst on two joyful souls.

A joyful smile covered three of them.

Smira was living her life to the fullest.

"*it was yesterday only when i craved to go outside and play with my friends, i was locked in my impalpable trap. But my so-called step mother did a right choice unknowingly. I got most lovable grandparents this month and two most enjoying friends, who never ever make me feel i am lonely. I wish that these days never ends. I want to hear frivolous rebukes of Ramiya and Erick, lectures from my grandparents.*"

After a moment,

Ramiya's mother came out after listening the noise.

She was about to say when Ramiya threw water on her as well. Her mother did not even bother and turned on the pipe lying down on the ground curled up like a snake,the splash of water touched Smira's face it felt like all her dark experiences are washing off those little droplets of water felt so refreshing. Ramiya's mother switched to her immature side and started living the moment. Smira had a smile *i wish i could have a mother like her.* Erick picked a pink water balloon followed by a yellow and a green one and he flexed his skills by jiggling those ballons. Ramiya looked at her mother and same was followed by her mother. Ramiya laughed,"this job perfectly suits you, Erick" Erick did not bother to give any attention to her words. "A joker! Next time wear the clown costu----" Yellow balloon burst on Ramiya's mouth.

Ramiya shouted,"YOU!!!" She ran to him to give a nice taste of death, Erick ran for his life.

Ramiya's mother laughed saying,"silly kids".

Smira loved the show, and this time too her dimples slew.

They were enjoying so hard that stopping the fun was irresistable.

Smira had a sudden thought she quickly ran inside the house and called grandparents. She took them outside.

But when they encounterred Ramiya and her mother, Their face got serious. Ramiya stopped her fun and her mother looked at the grass as if she wanted to say a lot but her mouth stopped the words.

Ramiya looked at them and then at Smira, Those doe eyes wanted Ramiya to get reunited with her grandparents. Ramiya then recalled what Smira told her at the amusement park, *they are lonely.*

Grandparents turned back and headed inside the house. Smira and Erick both were disappointed.

Then only soft hands held old hands of them they looked behind to find Ramiya holding their hands.

Resisting them to go.

Grandma and Grandpa looked at each other and then at Ramiya.

Tears filled their eyes. Recalling that what they all had experienced in the past,

Sun shone so brightly, "Miya!! look! our baby took her first step!" a proud and excited dad, enjoying his baby's first step.

Miya nodded with excitement.

'ding dong' bell rang.

"i will check who is on the door", Miya said. "it must be maa and papa." Ram added.

As Miya opened the door, she saw some tycoons standing.

She was confused, she said slowly,"who....are...y....."

"Where is he?"

Ram came and sweat overflew over him.

Miya was confused, figuring out what is going on!"

Those tycoon took him, Ramiya's father pretended to be cool, he smiled at Ramiya's mother and said,"everything is alright Miya!" his eyes shifted towards their newborn daughter.

He sighed and said,"give me 5 minutes". The tycoons said,"not more than that!" and they left.

Miya cried,"who are they!!" Ram said," it's nothing honey, just some business work."

"Have you decided what to name our beautiful daughter?" Miya smiled and said,"how could i? you are going to name our happiness!"

Ram said," see the time flew so quick! few days back, my happiness was all about us! i become super happy whenever we were together! but now whenever i see our daughter it's really equivalent to that happiness!" Miya smiled.

Ram checked the time.

"Miya.... The house in front of Maa and papa.... i have bought it.. so now that is our house!"

Miya smiled and said," that is a good thing Ram!! your wish came true!" Ram nodded.

smile on Miya's face converted in a frown face, "what about your brother....?"

Ram sighed.

He continued,"Because of him... i have lost so many things in my life, i can not live with my parents.. but i can afford to see them everyday, with legal rights."

Miya nodded and hugged him.

He looked at the time, only 10 seconds were left.

He quickly went to their daughter, whose eyes were so pretty that anyone could lost in them, cheeks so white and pink and rosy lips, which smiled seeing her dad. "Look she is smiling whenever you come close to her." Miya added.

Ram smiled and kissed her forehead. "You are so pretty my little girl!" Ram whispered.

Miya smiled.

Ram quickly stood up and hugged Miya, "you are the best wife... one could ask for! i hope you will be the best mother as well!" Ramiya nodded and said,"and you are going to be the best dad!"

Silence swooped.

"Miya i told you that i am so happy whenever we are together which is equivalent to whenever i see our daughter..."

"That's what i want.... Ram and Miya together...."

"Ramiya....... our daughter's name!"

Miya got excited, "Ram it is a good name!"

Ram said," Miya i guess my time is over, let me go see them."

Miya stood still with little Ramiya. Watching Ram leaving.

ಐ

Years passed... Miya started living with Ram's parents. It was a happy family only one missing was Ram.. Miya toil everyday in search of Ram, But it was her futile efforts.

"It is my 5th birthday maa! what are you going to gift me!" Ramiya asked. "what do you want my little monster..?" her mother asked so calmly.

"I want..... ummm leave it, i do not want anything right now!"

"MAA!! you tell me what you want!"

"Ramiya...." her mother tucked Ramiya's hair behind her ears and said softly," it's been 5 years... since your dad went missing, i hope he is fine and one day we all our going to celebrate. together."

Ramiya bit her lips,

Suddenly, Ram's brother and his wife came.

Miya stood up and said," hi! i was about to come downstairs."

"You don't need to come anywhere inside this house! you are going to leave this place as soon as possible!"

They were rude. very rude.

Ramiya's mother was confused. "Why are you being so harsh?"

"Come downstairs! and see it yourself!"

Ramiya looked at her mother.

They all came down.

Ramiya greeted her grandparents so excitedly," granny!! grandpa!!" Grandparents smiled and hugged her.

"WHO's birthday is today..?"

"Mine!"

"Ohh! look Miya!! our Ramiya is 4 now!" Miya smiled but then she looked at Ram's brother.

"I am 5 now!! granny!"

"ohh! big girl!!"

" Mom.. dad... i have called you because i have something very important to tell you all!"

Grandparents became serious.

Miya was confused.

After a bit of silence, Ram's brother said,"It's about Ram..."

Miya looked at him with big eyes. Grandparents became attentive now.

"Ram was not missing....."

Grandparents were serious they shouted," we are very possessif about Ram! so make yourself clear do not beat around the bush"

"Ram was not missing! he was DEAD!"

This was a great thunderclap to everyone! especially to Miya. She was mentally lost, tears fell from her eyes, a part of her was dead.

Ramiya was looking at everyone, she was confused.

Granny looked at Ramiya with tears, she said,"my baby.... go...play with Erick he was searching for you...."

Ramiya nodded, but she was uncomfortable in leaving her mother alone.

After she left, Grandpa said,"w...where is his...." he swallowed, it was hard to say this term.

Ram's brother smirked and said," you should ask this from Miya!"

Miya looked at him,"what are you talking about!". He came close to her," Miya murdered Ram! how could you do this Miya!! he fought with his family just for you! and you.... murdered him, the one who loved you the most in this world!"

Miya fell down.

Tears were impossible to stop.

thrill was running inside her, memories of Ram replayed in her mind and the fact that he is dead terrified her from top to bottom.

She wanted to speak so much but her mouth was not in her control,"how could you say that?"

"I do not need to clarify my statement to you! Mom! Dad, this woman has killed your son! are you still going to treat her as if she is our damn family member!"

Miya was lost in the thorny thought of Ram's death.

"KICK HER OUT OF OUR HOUSE"

Miya was now all broken, this much breakdown in a bit of time was inexplicable.

Miya was thrown out of the house, she was framed so disgustly.

She had no energy to proof herself, she cried so much.

A small and soft hand came and wiped her tears, it was Ramiya.

Miya hugged her so tight. And the dark night ended so harshly

They both hugged Ramiya.
Smira felt warm from afar.

She quickly came to Erick, excited and hi fived him.

Grand parents came to Ramiya's mother and said," we are really sorry hun."

Ramiya's mother's eyes met theirs.

Every word was so little at this situation, that a hug was the only option.

And their tears fade away in water when Erick threw water from pipe.

"IT IS THE BEST DAY!! LET US ALL ENJOY!!!"

XVI

"Our work is about to end, we will be free soon...from this shit" uncle Liz spitted out while pouring the liquid in a rich glass.

"Tell me when can i take Smira home with me!?"

"Do you know, What is day after tomorrow?"

-"no?"

"Tomorrow is Smira's birthday!"

-"Oh! how could i forget, that wrench was born on that day! haishhh"

"Tell me one thing, why are trapping Smira? She did not witnessed any of your crimes or any wrong doings. Then why?"

Smira's mother drank that liquid and came close towards uncle Liz, Her witchy eyes trapped uncle Liz's and with her long sassy red shiny nails she traced the glass and whispered " You do not need to know this, babe"

Uncle Liz, had an awkward laugh to balance this acidic situation.

Smira's mother made a serious face and said,"we will take Smira day after tomorrow!"

Uncle Liz nodded. Smira's mother had an evil Smirk.

Smira's mother woke up from her pretending sleep and looked at the sky from the window, it was very dark, even moon's light was covered with darkness and stars were impossible to spot. She went outside in the garden and started dialing.

"Hello.... are you there?"

-"hmm"

"Do you remember that some years back, i came to you for a help and you asked me to arrange an infant."

-"ohh.. so it's you... so is that kid now a teenager?"

"Yes, i will bring her to you the day after tomorrow."

-"Certainly, It is the best time! bring her i will arrange other things till then!"

"Finally! The diamond day is there! all these years i have longed for this day! soon i will be able to make it!"

Phone rings**

"Erick, pick up your phone! your ringtone is already so irritating".

"who cares about your point of view Rami!"

"Do not call me that you piece of shi---"

"Language! Ramiya!"

"But maa, have you heard what he said!?"

"Yes i did, Rami"

"Maaaaaa"

Erick spurted a laugh then his eyes encountered an innocent soul standing on the doorway.

He said," Ramiya do you know the meaning of pookie?"

Ramiya said,"ofcourse i know"

"look! who came.. Granny's pookie"

Ramiya saw Smira and welcomed her. Ramiya hit Erick's shoulder and said," stop your gibberesh!"

"Come Smira let us watch a cool movie!"

Smira's dimpled said hi to the environment, which made Everyone automatically smile.

She agreed and went with Ramiya giving side eye to Erick.

Erick had a sweet laugh.

Phone rings**

Erick again ignored it.

"How many times will you ignore your parent's call?" Ramiya's mother said while giving juice to him.

Erick hold the glass. Took a sip. He said," Sometimes i wish, i could have parents who undersatands me and gives me appropriate freedom! whom i can freely talk to!"

"Don't mind.. but i sometimes get jealous from Ramiya! She has the world's best mother!"

Ramiya's mother snorted out a laugh.

She winded up her work and sat beside Erick.

"I know that a child needs and ideal parent, which ofcourse is not so wrong! but the thing which most of the people agrees to that parents want ideal children."

"No parent wants to harm their child but they are not able to see the fact that child also need ideal parents."

"Believe me, i was never this free. I had never thought of being an easy mother! it was only Ramiya's father.."

Erick sensed that the conversation is heating up, he tried to change the topic.

"Aunt! you are amazing!"

Ramiya's mother smiled and said," Do not disrespect your parents! whenever they call you reply calmly!"

"Roger that!" Erick shouted and then smiled.

XVII

"Ramiya! What is going to happen? to...to..aaaaaaaaaaaa"

"Shhhh.. Don't be scared Smira! it is just a movie" said Ramiya hiding the fact that she is scared too.

Ramiya was trying so hard not to get scared, the plot came and television's power off button was clicked. simultaneously.

"That movie was bad!"

Smira laughed.

"Ramiya if you would have seen my lifestyle, you would have been so creeped out." Ramiya stood still.

"It was exactly like the movie."

Ramiya said,"Then you should click the power off button!"

"What is the power off button?" Smira asked.

"Umm.. it could be something that power off your step mother's plans"

Smira thought for a second.

Erick came inside.

Ramiya said," What are you doing here?"

Erick raised his brows and re-acted his acts, "I guess it is called 'coming inside a room'!"

Smira looked at him and laughed.

Ramiya said,"yo girl whose side are you!? huh?"
Smira controlled her pretty laugh.
"Yes granny's pookie! whose side are you? tell us?"
Smira looked at Erick and then at Ramiya.
"Is this even a question? obviously at Rami's side" Smira gulped.
Ramiya said," see..."
"WHAT!!!??"
"YOU too Smira!!!!!"
Erick laughed harder. Ramiya pushed him out.
Erick said," why are you guys boycotting me!?"
"It is a girl's dayout! We will play with you afterwards!"
Door shut.
"I should practice football with my bros then".
"But whom should i call first?"
"Let me call Michael first."
"Hello.... Michael!?"
--"yes?"
"are you free bro? let's play football?"
--"Right now i can't,I am with my family in boston."
"Oh..ok..."
"enjoy then, bye"
--"bye".
"Let ,me call someone else then.. umm yes jacob!"
"Hello Jacob, Are you free?"
--"I am not in the country"
"oh ok.. bye then"
"Now who..? yes! tim"
"hello..tim..? can you come to play football?"
--"bro... i wish! but i need to babysit my sister's friends"
"How long?"
--" umm i don't know.. how about you come over!?"
"OH... These girly stuff is not what a true man does. huh"

--"bye then.."

"How dare he hung my call like this. Well now i have no company."

Ramiya and Smira came out of the room.

Erick taunted,"now what!? you can't live a second without me! right?"

"What?" Ramiya was confused.

"Whatever" she said to herself and shouted,"Maaaa!! we are going to the mall!"

Erick had a jerk.

They both left.

"everyone is boycotting me." Erick frowned.

Smira came back to Erick.

"What?" Erick asked.

"Do you want to come..? with us?" Smira slowly asked with her innocent big eyes.

Erick got lost in them.

After a while,

He came back in senses and shouted "NO! I am going to hangout with my friends!"

Smira got Startled.

Ramiya came after hearing Erick's Loud words.

"Erick.. why are you shouting at her?"

Erick again shouted,"I have friends! I am going!" he left.

Ramiya said,"What happened to him?"

Smira looked at Ramiya and they both laughed.

"Let's go! I am going to buy you some cool stuff!"

Smira stood near ferris wheel, her hands holding shopping bags.

She looked here and there for Ramiya.

"Rami... where are you? it's scary being all alone. Please come fast."

Smira started walking slowly to find Ramiya.

"Freedom is over you brat!"

"no..no..no.. this can't be... she is not here! my mind is playing tricks. She cant-"

as Smira turned back, she was surprised. her body started shivering, her heart got heavy and she was bound with a wierd uncomfortable feeling.

"Did you miss me?" her mother smirked.

Shopping bags fell with a sudden jerk as she ran as fast as she could.

"hey! wait you bitch!" her mother got in her car and drove, following her. "Liz! we need to get her! or else we won't get the money! ugh! that bitch!"

While, Ramiya came by Ferris wheel looking for Smira. She stepped on one of the shopping bags, as her eyes moved down she got insane.

Her shaking fingers called her mother.

"hello?"

"m..maa!"

"What happened Rami?"

"S..Smira is lost"

"It's been months since i escaped my evil step mother, it's a relief but at the same time i feel bad for not having Ramiya and her family beside me. I really miss them"

"Sam.. Please close the store, I am leaving early.. got some work to do"

Smira nodded.

"I can not believe this is me! I never thought myslef to be independent. That day I left the town. Don't ask how. But luckily, i did it. I reached the city, They called New york City, Yes i am living solo in freaking NYC!

It's the part time job which keeps me healthy and fine, Thanks to Rhus.

Her story is a lot same to mine, the difference - Her Mother abandon her but i want mine to abandon me."

The bells jingle, Store's door opened and a cute yet handsome lad enterred.

" Sorry, The store is closing" Smira shouted as she untied her old dusty apron.

"That is a serious problem miss"

Smira looked at him. He smiled and both of his dimples said hi to her.

Smira got lost in them.

"Umm.. something wrong..?" He raised his eyes.

Smira shook her head,"Oh.. sorry, i am having this problem of zoning out"

"So You are saying that, I am boring?" he spurted out.

"No No! it's really not like that!" Smira argued, tension between her brows. "Chill, i was joking" he smiled.

"Myself, Alan" he offered a handshake.

Smira shook hands,"Smira."

"And that's when my life's countdown begin
   I liked Alan. Because he was sweet, he was nothing like my family, my evil mother, he was a comfort to me."

Smira was studying for her entrance exam. Some old lady adviced her to pursue law while she was buying eggplants and beans from the store.

Lamp on, Hairs tied in a pony, surrounded by papers and heavy books.

NOTIFICATION:

ALAN: Hi.. IMU ;}

Smira looked at her phone and smiled.

"All thanks to Ms. Amanda and Rami for teaching me how this little machine works."

ALAN: WHY ARE YOU IGNORING ME?

Smira sighed and resumed her work

"It's been a year since Alan and i got together, but i don't feel like myself with him, We also had a fight in this matter, but i can't help it. Things are different now, he is not the same as he was."

Her phone rang. She ignored.

buzz. again. ignored. again.

buzz.. buzz.. buzz.. buzz..

she picked up the call in frustration.

"WHAT THE HECK IS WRONG WITH YOU! I AM STUDYING RIGHT NOW! CAN'T YOU WAIT FOR SOME TIME!"

--------- "S....SMIRA....?" (SOBBNG)

Smira was still, "who..who is this..?"

"God!! I have missed you so much!!!"

Smira's eyes got watery, "R..Rami?"

"Where are you!!!"

Tears fall down her big innocent eyes."Ramiya.. i miss you a lot!"

Ramiya shouted,"wtf! Erik!! what are you doing!!"

Erik shouted back,"i also want to talk to dadi's pookie!! i found her number!"

Ramiya,"FINE!"

Erik,"hello!! Dadi's pookie... where are you!! we are coming right now!"

Smira smiled, her dimples could be seen.

"I am in NYC"

Ramiya and Erick hooted. "SMIRA! GIRL! NYC! text us the address we will be there!"

Smira,"Hmm.. I love you both! and i miss you so much!" phone cut.

> *"I recalled days with Rami and Erick everyday, every second. They make me happy, i feel joyful and myself with them. FRIENDS. yes, they make us feel like ourselves."*

ALAN: WE ARE MEETING TOM. SERIOUS DISCUSSION!

> *"Unlike some random people we chose to spend rest of life just because you felt alone or you felt the need to be with somebody."*

೮೦

Smira woke up, new day and a happy one. Sunshine kissed her cute deep dimples, She opened her eyes and stretched her body. The day started like a song, of happy reincarnation.

She came out of the bathroom, wore a cute pink dress with tiny white butterflies all over and tied her hair in a pony, she sprayed her favourite perfume and went in hurry picking her bag and locking her flat.

She called Ramiya,"hi.. are you there?"

Ramiya replied," About to reach..."

Smira smiled,"see you..."

She kept the phone in her bag and ran towards the cafe.

"SMIRA!" Alan shouted. Smira bit her tongue as she turned.

"A..Alan..."

"What is your problem!? why can't you just talk to me nicely! huh!?"

Smira looked down. scared.

"NOW SAY SOMETHING!"

"A...Alan.. i think we should end..."

He held her hand forcefully"COMPLETE THAT FREAKING SENTENCE! AND YOU ARE DEAD!"

"It's hurting..." Smira cried.

"WOAH WOAH COOL DOWN BUDDY" Ramiya exclaimed.

Smira looked up, and Ramiya was actually there, Standing wearing her 'all time favs' - jeans, and a tight t shirt, holding shopping bags in one hand and the other hand behind.

Alan turned back," who are you!?"

Ramiya took out pepper spray from her pocket and sprayed it.

Alan shouted," ARE YOU MAD! YOU BITCH!" he ran away.

Smira and Ramiya laughed, but Smira knew he would come back. This time with more aggression.

Ramiya hugged smira with one hand,"girl.. i missed you.." Smira got very happy, seeing Ramiya.

☙

The fresh scent of rain on dry earth was intoxicating. There was warmth and secure aura which was engulging Smira as she sat on soft seat in the cafetria - her favourite. Crowd huming, raindrops falling down the window, making pitter patter sound.

The place was filled with vanilla and coffee scent all over with a tint of best reunion with favourite people.

"So Smira! who tf was that guy?" Ramiya argued eating pizza.

Smira cleared her throat and saw Ramiya, eating with no manners, just like she used to do in the past. Smira was reliefed. She felt as if she found the missing piece whose absence affected her peace and happiness for months.

Ramiya snapped her fingers, "Smira! tell me!"

Smira looked down and cracked her knuckles,"Ummm.. eh..."

"Well he is my boyfriend." Smira finally let it out in one go.

"DUDE! NO! SHIT!" Ramiya coughed out with the last slice of pizza in her mouth. She drank cold drink,"That bastard was humiliating you, girl! you have to end this bullshit!" Ramiya ordered.

Smira exhaled.

"Rami... I tried, I literally did! but he is forcing me, for staying in this hell."

"First it was my mother, then him." Smira let out a sarcastic laugh while making circles on the empty plate with a random cuttlery.,"This Impalpable Trap won't leave me ever. I don't know where are the keys! how to find them!?"

Ramiya looked at her, and feed her a slice of pizza."Smira! i will help you! no matter what! this time, i am not leaving you for a bit!"

Smira smiled, eating pizza.

"Again! y'all forgot me!" Erick pulled the seat and sat while eating fries from Ramiya's plate.

Ramiya hit his hand. Smira laughed.

"I missed you all!" Smira cried.

ॐ

""

"After Ramiya and Erick left, I blocked Alan and started ghosting him. I go insane thinking about what will he do? he isn't safe! but right now i have to prepare for my entrance exam. It's the only way to get rid of The trap! which follows me."

XIX

NOTIFICATION:

ALAN: LET'S END THIS. MEET ME NEAR YOUR HOUSE.

"*My gutt said no to his offer, but it's high time! i can't live with this torture and blackmailing. It's been four months since he is threatening me, saying he will tell my evil mother about me.*

(PROTIP: NEVER TELL A BOY ABOUT YOUR DEEP SECRETS)

*I went outside, and this time i was nervous. I wore my cozy pajamas, when i reached the place he asked me to come, I saw him. Anger in his eyes, aggression in his body, he came towards me. rapidly. And i was scared. to the fullest. He shouted, "what do you want!" i was numb, which made him more angry. "WHAT DO YOU WANT!" he shouted and this time, with a lot of pressure his hand hit my cheek. **shit**. this man, slapped me.*

and my mind got lost in the series of question, who is this person? who gave him the right to control my decision? who gave him the right to control my life? who gave him the right to threaten me? who gave him the right to hit me!?

my heart shattered into pieces.

That day was one of those horrible days.

Tomorrow is my entrace exam."

&

"After i came home from the exam centre, i saw Alan's message, "I have told your mother about you bitch! You broke my heart! I won't let you lead a happy life! Not in this lifetime!"

This was it. The thing i was most scared of."

"I wish he dies! UGH! What have he done!"

Doorbell rings, Smira was conviced that it's the end of her story, her eyes saw a knife lying on the kitchen range. She walked slowly towards the door and took that knife for self defence, sweat dripping her forehead, Her footsteps so light as if they were feathers. She reached the door and stretched her arm to unlock the door, She closed her eyes and opened the door.

As she opened the door, It was Grandpa and Grandma. She opened her eyes and sighed deeply.

Smira throwed the knife and without thinking anything for a bit she hugged them.

Grandparents brought sweets, chocolates, a beautiful phone charm and a of dress which was in her wishlist and it's no doubt who told them about her wishlist- Erick. Grandparents shrugged and saw each other as Smira hugged them both and started crying,"Smira.. look you have grown up a lot dear.."

"I love you both!" Smira sobbed.

"Oh.. child..." Grandma's brows knitted.

"Wow, now anyone cares about me or i am just for granted!?" Erick said bluntly from behind holding all the bags.

"Erick I know, You found me... It's because of you i met Rami , grandpa and grandma!"

Erick smiled.

Smira wiped her tears and in great excitement, she said "Let's go for a tour!"

౬౨

"Grandma! Grandpa! see this is the store, where i do my part time job. The owner is so kind she allows me to study for the exam without making any changes in my salary."

"That's so kind of her." grandma pat Smira's back.

"Let's go to the fair! It's been few days i gotta know about it, i wanted to go there so badly." Smira exclaimed.

Grandpa laughed," If our Smira wants to go we are going there. definitely!" Smira's dimple said hi to everyone.

Erick whispered,"HI"

Smira was confused, she looked back no one was there. She replied,"HI.. wierdo"

Erick got a jerk,"wh...what did you say to me!!! WIERD-O!!!?"

"Listen! you grandma's pookie! I said hi to your dimples, which i am sure were not seen all these months. And just because you started living your own life doesn't mean you will say gibberish to me!"

Smira looked down in guilt. Erick looked at grandparents. Grandparents actioned him to apologies. Grandpa broke the awkward silence,"Me and your grandma are going first, we will wait for you two with tickets, bring some icecream" and they left.

Erick clears his throat to break the awkward silence after grandparents left.

"umm..mm.. sorry." Erick spitted looking here and there.

Smira looked at him and smiled.

Erick looked at her and smiled back.

"first lets take ice cream" Smira walked ahead.

"wait for me!" Erick ran behind her.

After walking some distance, Smira asked,"How did you find me?"

Erick looked ahead as if he was reminscing the time when Smira left,"I don't know.. when you left we all were worried, Ramiya thought it's because of her. There were no happiness in the house. So i had to do something, to find you. So i did some serious research..."

Smira looked at him, stared deeply into his soul.

"Haish.. OKAY.. I found you through social media and took your number from Rhus."

Smira shook her head and laughed so badly.

Erick looked at her and laughed too.

"You are insane. Erick!" Smira hit his head.

"woah.. you have really changed yourself." Erick argued.

Smira smiled. Her phone buzzed, she checked her phone and saw the message from Alan. Again Absurd.

Smira sighed.

Erick saw the tension hugging Smira.

"Just block him." Erick mentioned casually.

Smira looked at him, tensed and stressed.

"He is my ex.." Smira started the story with this,

"WHAT THE-!" Erick was speechless,"Smira! he is your what!?"

Smira was embarassed.

"I don't know, at that time i was surrounded by the feeling of being with someone, i have never been felt loved."

Erick looked at her and got serious,"look he seems like a sociopath. Ignore him. There's a best solution for this problem."

Smira listened carefully,

"You can come to granny's place! you can start your new life there with Rami, Granny, Grandpa, Aunt Mia! you will get a beautiful family and you don't have to worry about college. Aunt Mia will plead to the central university to give you admission in our town"

Smira analysed Erick's Advice.

"I will look into it. Thanks Erick!"

Erick smiled and ran,"the person who reached icecream shop first gets one more ice cream"

Smira ran and shouted,"It's me. The Winner."

XX

"

It's been days, since he is texting me absurd messages. He invaded my social media and he even changed my username to slutt. So cheap. Today is my result, and i am nervous, Grandma had told me that i will get the admission, her trust in me was so pure. I can't wait to live with them. Again. Yes, I decided to take Erick's advice and packed my bags.

I have packed almost everything. I just have to lock my flat and handover the keys.

Let's say goodbye to my dear little flat.

Door bell rang, It must be Erick.

i went to open the door,"

"HI! DID YOU MISS MOMMY?"
"BACK TO THE PRISON BITCH!"

"Maa! Smira is coming back! i am very happy!" Ramiya exclaimed.

Ramiya's mother is decorating the house with lights and flowers.

Erick walked in, eating popcorns.

Ramiya shouted,"Why are you still here!? Smira must be waiting!"

Erick put a handfull of popcorns in his mouth," I am just leaving..."

Ramiya shouted, "AAAA!!"

Erick and her mother had a jumpscare,"what happened?"

"Today, her result will be out! let me check!" she quickly ran to the living area, where a whole meal was served for Smira. She grabbed her phone and enterred the information.

"AAAA!!" She shouted again.

"What is it this time!?" Erick asked.

"She got her admission! She will be a lawyaer!! OUR SMIRA! Is going to be a Lawyer!"

Her Mother got a relief and she smiled," Rami.. call her and give her the good news!"

Ramiya called Smira, call was transferred to voicemail.

Ramiya,"GIRL! You aced the exam! we all are proud of you! Come home fast! Can't wait any longer!"

ಎ

Smira heard Ramiya's voicemail,lying on the floor, blood flowing sevrely, her eyes closing down slowly.

"I never knew my death will look like this. I wore my Favorite and expensive dress, which is now stained

RED. I had imagined, Grandma complementing my dress while Erick making fun of it, Ramiya hitting him because she can't resist taking my side. Ramiya's mother being the best mother ever and grandpa protecting the whole family. That bastard took it all, it's my fault. I gave him the permission to do this shit. I don't know where i am going now, but I am glad that i am dying, there won't be my step mother's evil plan and my ex's tortured threats, I will be safe with god. Finally i found the key for my trap, I am out of the impalpable trap! but i will miss you so much Rami."

Tears fell from her eyes and got mixed with her blood, as her eyes closes - *forever*

THANKYOU

WE ALL MAKE MISTAKES

In this world, we get engaged with people who turns out to be a sicko. And it's alright, its not your fault! It's not you who is the culprit here. It's not your problem that the person have mental abnormilities.

Although that person isn't safe and does everything to bring you down, you don't have to feel insecure. You are enough to deal with these scumbags. We live in a world where the democracy is only for Men, while We Women are just supporters.

It's so true, Women are Unsafe within the house and Out of the house. And despite being many movies, stories or inspirational videos, Men don't get it. They will not stop doing whatever their libido asks them to do while, we have to control our unconsciousness.

All The Ladies out there, Remember you are STRONG, ENOUGH and DEFENSIVE.

Thankyou for reading my book till the last, Wait for the next volume of Impalpable trap.

I hope you enjoyed reading.

You can share your feedback on my instagram account, @sheischaotic

THANKYOU!